LET HER REST NOW

VIJAY NAIR is the author of *The Boss is Not Your Friend* (a work of non-fiction), *Master of Life Skills* (fiction) and *The Gloomy Rabbit and Other Plays*. His essays have been included in international anthologies. A recipient of the Fulbright Senior Research Grant and the British Council Charles Wallace Award, he was also awarded a US State Department Grant to attend the International Writers' Program at the University of Iowa. He lives in Bangalore with his wife and son. He can be reached at vijay@vijaynair.net.

W0246982

Let Her Rest Now

Vijay Nair

hachette
INDIA

First published in 2012 by Hachette India
(Registered name: Hachette Book Publishing India Pvt. Ltd)
An Hachette UK company
www.hachetteindia.com

SRD

ISBN 978-93-5009-282-8

Hachette Book Publishing India Pvt. Ltd
4th/5th Floors, Corporate Centre,
Plot no. 94, Sector 44, Gurgaon 122003, India

Typeset in Berthold Baskerville 11/14.1
by InoSoft Systems Noida

Printed and bound in India
by Manipal Technologies Limited, Manipal

MIX
Paper | Supporting
responsible forestry
FSC™ C043100

For Seema & Anju,
Friends in Distant Lands...

If you had told me...

First the traffic, then the forest with the monkeys, then a herd of elephants, then a lone bison – the world turns beautiful as I leave it behind. The rain that was a mere trickle half an hour ago is a steady downpour in these parts, washing the trees and turning the leaves a lush, glistening green. The sly creeks in the hills are small waterfalls that gurgle their jest. The road is treacherous now with 'Careful, Hairpin Bend Ahead' signs that slow us down. Man and Nature have conspired to gift travellers a longer time to take in the breathtaking view.

I have taken this road many times as a child.

It used to feel ominous during those days; a painful reminder that the home I shared with my mother during the holidays was being left behind.

An old familiar ache takes over, priming me for the restless nights and the relentless jibes and bullying of the older children in the days that, once, lay ahead.

We grow up. We don't learn to forget.

The driver is moved by Nature's elegance. He has discarded the sullenness he had affected after I reprimanded him for trying to overtake a bus in the new four-way linking Bangalore with Mysore, and almost getting us squashed by the angry man at the wheel in the process. Drivers of hired cabs almost always try this on unsuspecting passengers at the start of a journey. To test how far they can be pushed.

The driver wants to know the purpose of my visit. Do I have family living here? He looks dissatisfied when I tell him I have work in Coonoor. I have caught him checking me out in the rear-view mirror many times. I am not surprised. I am hardly the sort of a passenger he ferries routinely from the congestion of the city to the starkness of the hills. I have refused to step out of the car for lunch even though it has been nearly five hours since we started from Bangalore.

I must have appeared all the more vulnerable to him; a young woman, picked up from the airport and making a seven-hour road trip alone. My petite frame and the confusion I customarily carry in my eyes makes me fair game for all types of men. Drivers of cabs and auto-rickshaws, bus-conductors, cinema-hall ushers, Delhi eve-teasers and sometimes even vegetable vendors, think they can take liberties with me. The malls with branded clothing lines that endorse empowered women in business suits might have sprung up in the cities but the man in the street still wants to punish me for walking and travelling unaccompanied. He is usually outraged when I refuse to take the bullying lying down.

My appetite for grief is insatiable. I have cried for most part of the trip. Not expansively. Not in large heaving sobs.

But the tears have flown unrestricted as small hamlets and villages have sped by. There is no way he doesn't know, that as I sit behind him, I have given myself to unmitigated sorrow. Thankfully, he has not tried to make conversation until now. After I have composed myself enough to ask him how much longer it's going to take us to reach.

The handful of people who had turned up afterwards had commended me for being strong. I had quietly gone about attending to all the chores that death brings in its wake. And hers had been a particularly messy one. Even the police had played a part in the funeral arrangements. The presence of pesky journalists hadn't helped. When you decide to go like that you don't just lose your life, you lose the right to any privacy that you had a claim to when you were alive.

My mother, after all, had made the cardinal sin of getting herself murdered.

For a long time after her death all I could feel was an enormous rage directed at her. I stayed up nights thinking she had brought the violence on herself. If she had been a different person and led a different life, it wouldn't have happened. Respectable folks don't get killed like that. And didn't the murdered always invite the brutal retribution? They lied, they cheated, they blackmailed, bringing out the worst in others. I knew my mother was capable of all that. Who better than me to testify against her way of life? I knew everything that she had kept hidden from the world. Her shrewd appraising gaze that could sum up what a person was worth in a matter of minutes. The way she could figure out what she would be able to extract from a person. Her ruthless streak when it came to realizing her own agenda. She was incapable of giving unconditionally. I was the only exception to the rule and, ironically enough, I had never wanted anything from her. Love always demands reciprocity and I had not been able to love her for a long time, at least not in the way she wanted me to.

Despite the anger, I resolutely made the trips to Lucknow to meet the cops, even after I realized that they were not so much interested in finding out who had killed her as they were in digging out all the salacious details of her personal life. Worse, they seemed to be more titillated than horrified by the crime. More than one of them had been eager to supply the details about the circumstances in which she had been found.

I repeatedly heard from them that her face, battered to pulp, had been caked with blood. The murderer had bashed in her face so brutally that one of her eyes had nearly fallen out. Her hands had been tied in front, in a gesture of supplication, as if owning responsibility for having invited such a death.

I did not see her like that. They had worked on her in the mortuary and made her somewhat presentable. But in my nightmares she always appears as the cops described her.

They all made the same statement with little variation: 'She was living alone but everyone in the city knew of her connections.'

After her violent death, my murdered mother amounted to nothing more than the set of powerful connections she had – though none of them were around to put pressure on the authorities to investigate the crime more thoroughly. The proverbial rats had deserted the sunken ship.

And that included the man.

He was the one to discover her body. Or so I believed. After all, it was he who had called me from the phone in my mother's house. He who told me that she had met with an accident and that I should leave for Lucknow as soon as possible. I knew from the tone of his voice that there was more to the accident. Somehow I knew as soon as I had finished speaking to him that I wouldn't see her alive again.

He wasn't around when I reached Lucknow. In fact, I didn't meet him on that trip at all. He called once in those days to tell me that it was best if he stayed away as the media was impatient for scoops. 'There are others who can get hurt in all this.' Others meant his family. The legitimate one. One wife. Two sons. One daughter. And a large dog. They were all accommodated in the family photograph I spotted in the Sunday supplement of a leading newspaper that had carried a story on politicians of royal blood a few weeks after the murder. I am sure he had got a journalist crony of his to do the story. To make the gullible world believe he was a family man and any speculation to the contrary owed to his jealous political rivals – and not because it had any basis in reality.

I had placed the newspaper on my bedside table; it was a painful reminder. My eyes were drawn to the photograph every night before I tried to sleep. I didn't look like any of them. I had taken after my mother. Still, I desperately sought a connection, even though I knew that if I ever ran into any of them in a public place they would either not recognize me – or not want to.

My weekend trips to Lucknow stopped after I saw that picture. Along with my yearning to be a part of the photograph, the awareness that my mother and the man had been having a lot of fights in the months preceding her death had settled in. On my last visit, before she died, I had heard her arguing bitterly with him on the phone. That realization led to a new fear. Did he have anything to do with her being bumped off? Had she turned into an inconvenience for him? I was terrified at the possibility. If he were to be nabbed as the killer, the hints and the innuendo in the media reports would turn it into a front-page scandal leaving me with no place to hide.

And I have spent all my adult years wanting to hide.

After my trips to Lucknow stopped I had found myself an expensive shrink. She had kind eyes and a shy smile. Week after week I went to her to pour my heart out. To tell her my story. To find out from her why I couldn't rid myself of the rage I felt towards my mother even though she was no longer around for me to vent it on her. To understand why I was unable to shed a single tear at her loss. To figure out how I could maintain the facade of 'all's well' at work while storms raged within.

I dropped out of counselling after a few months when I realized that all the sessions were designed to lead to the same outcome. Session after session, she tried to gently point out to me that I was like my mother in many ways and in order to heal I had to forgive her.

I didn't know how to do that and the impassive shrink sitting behind an even more impassive table could offer no suggestion in this regard.

I had to concede she was a waste of time.

The only thing that had helped was work. The office I worked in was no different from other organizations. Many make friends with those they work with, but people like me make it clear we come to work because we are paid to. Since making friends is not a part of the brief, we are happy to smile and exchange pleasantries with those who work with us and ignore the rest. Sharing family secrets is not part of the deal.

The newspapers in the capital had carried a small piece on the inside pages. One of them hinted at Mother's alliance with a powerful minister in UP. Even if her death had been announced more prominently, I doubt anyone at work would have made the connection. My face gave nothing away. I was always dressed staidly in business suits when I went to work. My hair was cut short and apart from a dab of pale lipstick there wasn't a hint of make-up on my face. They say children own up to the disowned parts of their parents. My mother and I were exception to the rule. She had owned up to any wild streak I may have possessed. And I had inherited the sobriety I don't think she knew she possessed.

Before leaving on that fateful day I had called Prerna, a colleague, and asked her to inform my boss, Pulkith. He was in London and I couldn't get hold of him on the phone.

Prerna and I often had lunch together at work when we weren't travelling. It was a comfortable relationship but we weren't friends and that kept my voice from cracking when she told me softly to take care and not worry about anything.

No one intruded my space when I got back to work, maintaining a respectful distance. Only Pulkith and

Prerna asked a few careful questions before offering their condolences. I was grateful for the sensitivity and immersed myself in my work, clocking twelve hours on most working days.

It's strange how grief has found me after so many months. There is something about this journey that has made me go back to the days when innocence was still present in my life, unfettered by the filters of adult judgement through which I had viewed my mother in later years. Somehow the car journey brought back happier moments we had shared. Like the holidays and shopping trips she took me for when I was younger. She used to cuddle me a lot until I reached my teen years and put an end to that practice.

Maybe the tears are flowing because it's another death that is taking me back to the place where I spent most of my childhood. Another woman has been killed. A stranger. This time it is not the dead but the living who want my presence.

Samir is in police custody. They believe he killed her. According to his mother, the only person he wants to talk to is me. She called me yesterday to relay the message from her son. After my mother, Samir is the only one who comes close to being family. I don't want to lose him too.

I took the first flight from Delhi to Bangalore this morning after I was told that all the flights to Coimbatore were full.

It's almost dark by the time we reach the cottage. We have driven past the hotel and the deserted church where Samir and I used to rest after the walk up the hill. The lone bulb hanging from the porch illuminates the carefully tended garden resplendent with flowers of every conceivable colour. Samir is a painter. He has always loved flowers. When we were in school, he spent all his free time with the gardener, learning about natural pigments and dyes that he could use for his paintings. I pay off the driver and add an extra two hundred as his tip. He looks at me and smiles. We are at ease with each other now that the journey is over.

Vrinda opens the door. She's as beautiful as she has always been. Every time I meet her, I am struck by the resemblance between mother and son. Especially after Samir grew up and lost all his baby fat. They share the very fair complexion that hints at a foreign bloodline. Samir had told me once that his great-grandmother was Belgian. Mother and son look at the world with the same sleepy eyes flecked grey-black. It's in the mouth that their faces differ. Samir has a more generous one. It doesn't take much to make him smile. Vrinda is more guarded. Maybe she has never learnt to trust.

'You have come,' Vrinda whispers, her hand reaching out tentatively to touch my face in a gesture of rare affection.

'I wish I could have been here earlier,' I blurt out, a little overwhelmed by how vulnerable Vrinda is looking at that moment. 'All the flights to Coimbatore were full.'

'It must be because of the big industrial fair that started there today. Now they won't allow you to meet him until tomorrow in the afternoon,' she says resignedly and then composes herself. 'Do you want some tea? I made some pork pickle sandwiches for you. The ones you used to love when the two of you visited me from school.'

'Thank you, I am famished,' I tell her. 'Somehow I couldn't bear to have lunch on the way.' Both of us are trying hard to bring a semblance of normalcy to our words. To postpone the inevitable conversation we must have about Samir and where he is right now. It is not fair on either of us. Especially Vrinda. Women should not be forced to seek help from the friends of their children. I start to get angry. For how long does Samir expect others to clear up the mess he creates?

'I really don't think he had anything to do with this,' Vrinda pries into my thoughts. As usual she has been canny enough to read them and can't wait to tell me that what I am tempted to believe about her son is wrong. When I was younger, this trait of hers used to frighten me. My mother could never intrude into my head like Vrinda did. Maybe Ma immunized herself from the very beginning. Maybe she didn't want to know what I was thinking; she was always scared of my thoughts.

Vrinda can take that liberty with me. After all she can't be held responsible for anything that's happened in my life. When she leaves me alone in the guest room, I wonder whether she dares to be as perceptive about her own son. Mothers learn their defences early. They want to believe that their children live in the world they have created for them. I am sure that in the space Vrinda had imagined her son occupying, getting arrested for a heinous crime had not been factored in.

She arranges the plate of sandwiches on the table and pours me a cup of tea. 'I would have liked you to stay with Randeep and me in the club but I thought that they would realize by this morning that it was all a mistake and release

Samir. I was planning a celebratory lunch for all of us. It would have been a nice surprise for him to find you in the cottage when he came home. But it has been the kind of a day when everything goes wrong. They told me yesterday that they had taken in Samir only for questioning. But this morning they formally arrested him. The whole thing is made more complicated by the fact that Karla's house does not fall under the jurisdiction of the police station of this town. And the cops out there are being really unreasonable. But we are going to get him out...' Vrinda chatters on and on. I have never heard her talk so much. Her words are clouded by an unarticulated fear.

I tell myself Vrinda will succeed in getting Samir out of this mess. She always gets whatever she sets her mind on.

She is that kind of a woman.

Karla, the murdered woman, was Vrinda's friend. They were together at school in Dehradun. Everyone in Samir's family seems to have had their initial education in boarding school. The irony of it strikes me later when Vrinda has retired for the night after sharing with me what she knew about the murder and how her son got implicated in the mess.

I was banished to a boarding school far away from home because Mother was my only family. The man came over only sometimes and stayed the night. On the mornings I met him, he rarely acknowledged me. I was sent to the hostel when I was six.

Memories decide for you what you choose to carry from them. I don't recall much of the life I had with my mother before I was packed off to the distant hill-station.

I know the man must have had something to do with it. I must have been an inconvenience when he sought out my mother to entertain his party colleagues. He paid all the bills, though. I am sure Mother insisted on this. Irrespective of how much he disliked having me, he could not have evaded the responsibility of having to take care of me. Not that it could have been much of a burden for him. His family has adapted to modern ways by choosing politics as their vocation. That means he has loaded bank accounts stashed away all around the world – without having done a single day's honest work.

One day I asked my mother, 'Didn't my father want me?' We were driving back from one of the short holidays she insisted on taking with me when I came home on vacation.

'No,' she said and looked away.

There was nothing more to be said.

I had always thought Samir had been sent to the hostel because his parents had decided to separate. It's only after Vrinda talked of her friendship with the murdered woman that I realized Samir would have spent his childhood in a hostel irrespective of whether his parents had been together or not. His family believed it was supremely important to banish the child from the fold for a dozen years in the cause of education. They have done so for generations.

There are things about Samir I don't know even though we have been best friends for years. The thought gnaws at me and I start crying softly again.

Just before a fitful sleep claims me, I recall faintly the words of Kalpana, the shrink I used to go to, explaining something called a 'delayed stress reaction'.

The first feeling I am greeted with on waking up is guilt. Samir and I became friends when we were in Class VII. Before that, we were ensconced with our own gender. Boys were anathema to me. I guess it was natural that being rebels we would gravitate towards each other once we grew up and the teachers started keeping a hawk-eye on boys and girls getting too close for their comfort. We exchanged notes on the books and music we loved, shared our first crushes with each other and for a brief while even turned into 'boyfriend/ girlfriend' in the parlance of our peers. It didn't last. Both of us learnt soon enough that passion and friendship don't mix. But we made a pact when we left school. We were always going to be there for each other.

I certainly am not with him tonight. I am sleeping comfortably in his house while he is slumming it in the police lock-up.

It is the persistent knocking on the door that makes me get up reluctantly from my bed. Vrinda is standing at the door with a tea tray. She has dark circles under her eyes. It's clear she hasn't slept the whole night. 'Did you get any sleep at all? Your face is all puffy,' is her greeting to me.

I want to tell her she too is looking stressed. But the wan smile she gives me is enough for me to understand she knows what I want to say. She says she is leaving for the club and meeting her husband in an hour. He had accompanied her the day before but had left for Chennai as soon as he'd found out about the arrest to arrange a good lawyer for his stepson.

Samir's real father is in the Himalayas. Soon after he was divorced from Vrinda, he left for an ashram in Himachal

Pradesh. He lives there now and is not in touch with anyone from his family. Including Samir. I guess however different our lives have been, that's one thing I am always going to share with my best friend. Both of us have fathers who brought us into this world and then decided to wash their hands off us.

Vrinda changed things for Samir by gifting him with a new father when we were in our final year of school. I was the only friend Samir invited to the wedding.

I had always thought Samir was luckier than me. Now I am not so sure. Who among the two of us was dealt the better hand? In all this, is Samir the only one getting punished? After all, if he is hanged for murdering that woman, I will lose the only anchor I have left in my life.

Why am I always the chosen one?

I would have known

Samir refuses to look up. He has been sitting on a stool and staring at the ground since the time he was escorted into the meeting room by a constable. He looks gaunt. The stubble on his face and his sleep-deprived eyes make him look much older. Vrinda has brought along her husband and a lawyer. The room is too small to hold the five of us. Everyone barring me has tried to coax some answers from him.

Samir has steadfastly refused to speak.

'Maybe we should just leave him with Neha. He wanted to speak to her.' There is no sign from Samir that he has heard his mother. They all troop out of the room. The lawyer throws me a speculative look on his way out. He probably thinks I'm an accomplice.

As if he has been waiting for just this moment, Samir looks up at me and mumbles something. I can't hear him and lean in closer.

'I swear, Neha, I had nothing to do with either of them. I would never think of harming...' he bursts into tears before he can finish.

'Oh Samir…what's happened to you?' I can't recognize my own voice. I step forward and gather him in my arms. We are both crying now. We have done this before. In our last few years at school, I used to come back after every holiday and have at least one crying bout in his presence. Samir used to call it my 'comeback performance' but he used to join in the crying after some time. This is probably the first time he has initiated the theatrics and I have followed suit.

I am not sure how long we hold each other before there is a knock and Vrinda enters. 'They are saying visiting hours are over.'

I draw away from Samir and look at her uncertainly.

She tries to smile at me and then moves towards her son. 'Mr Krishnamachari is the best criminal lawyer in Chennai. He says he will make sure that you get bail. But you have to talk to him, Samir; being silent like this will only make things worse for you.'

Samir resumes his stoic yogi-like stance. He refuses to meet his mother's eyes. She sighs, looking at me. We leave the room together, almost colliding with the stern policeman who appears in an obscene hurry to take the prisoner back to his cell.

On the drive back to the cottage, the lawyer wants to know if Samir has told me anything at all. I am in a quandary. Meeting Samir has taken me back to our years in school when we had both forged a 'don't tell' pact. All the secrets we shared were not meant for anyone else. It used to infuriate all his girlfriends. Not just in school but afterwards too.

'You have to tell him,' Vrinda cuts in impatiently. 'We need every bit of information we can lay our hands on to get Samir out of there.'

I can strangle her for once again intuiting my reluctance. 'He didn't say much,' I respond. 'All he said was that he was not responsible for either of them.'

'*Either* of them? Are you sure he said that?' The lawyer has a grating voice. I am sure just his tone is enough to intimidate judges to rule in his favour.

'Yes. That's what I remember him saying.'

'But you were in there for nearly forty minutes. Surely he said other things too?' Samir's stepfather interjects smoothly.

I shake my head. It is throbbing. There's something else Samir said inside the room. But I have shut it out. My memory is getting more selective by the day. All I can remember is the way Samir and I held each other. There was a comfort in that hug that nothing else in life can give me.

'So what were you doing inside all that time?' The man is clearly displeased.

'Crying,' I admit rather shamefacedly.

'I find it interesting that he said *either of them*. It means there's more than one death that we have to take into account,' says Krishnamachari after a long pause. Clearly the observant lawyer deserves the fat fee he charges his clients.

I look out of the window. The hills are arrogant in their beauty, carrying strips of clouds on their heads.

'Did you ferret out any information from the inspector?' Samir's stepfather butts in again. The tone of his voice suggests he is really worried and wants to cling to any straws he can find.

'Well, he said the victim was not only murdered brutally and that her face was all bashed in but that the murderer had positioned her hands in a gesture of contrition and tied them in front. Making her look as if she wanted to be pardoned for what *he* had done!'

'You are assuming the murderer is a man,' Vrinda says dryly.

The lawyer turns around from the front seat to look at her. 'The brutality of the crime seems to suggest that.'

She shakes her head in exasperation. 'How readily we jump to conclusions. Is a woman not capable of bashing in another woman's face after killing her and tying up her hands?'

Although I have not been paying attention to what is being said, the last few words cut through my thoughts. I am unable to breathe. The blood rushes to my temples. I see myself falling from the edge of a steep cliff.

Samir and my mother adored each other. There were times in the past when the three of us were together and I had felt like an intruder in their space. I remember throwing a major tantrum about it when I was fourteen. The two of them had taught me that it's always those we rely on the most who have the power to inflict maximum hurt. My mother certainly made a habit of causing me pain with the life she led. Samir compounded it by unconditionally supporting her in whatever she said or did.

Life and irony are interchangeable. There were times when I have wanted to kill both of them. Now I am confronted with the possibility that one of them murdered the other.

Before my mother died, I had been in a relationship. Subbu was a good Tamil Brahmin boy and for a long time pretended to be someone that he was not. The effort tired him out eventually and he left to marry a nice Iyengar girl of his parents' choice. We were living together in a small flat in Vasant Vihar and he didn't stay long enough to say goodbye in person. Instead he left me a note on the dining table.

> *Dear Neha,*
>
> *I am sure you have seen this coming for some time. I don't see a future for us. Last time I went to Madras, Amma insisted I meet this girl. Latha is from our community and a chartered accountant by profession. My parents think she is a perfect match for me.*
>
> *I don't know whether there is any point in telling you that I will always love you. But I also know we can never be happy together. I am never going to know where I stand with you. And for you I am always going be a poor compensation for Samir.*
>
> *I may as well make my parents happy.*
> *Love,*
> *Subbu*
>
> *PS. I have put the 10k I borrowed from you inside the pouch in the locker. Thanks for everything.*

The letter had made me so angry that I called Subbu to tell him I hoped his accountant wife could put up with his disgusting drooling when he slept. I added that I was glad that he had taken the initiative in the matter as I was about to call it off myself. To make him feel worse I also told him that I had literally begged my organization to give me a project that made me travel only to avoid the prospect of coming back home to him. All of it was true – what hurt was that he had the courage to call it quits while I had struggled with the decision for months.

'So long as you are happy,' he had said in a small voice before hanging up.

Afterwards I had spoken to Samir to complain how all my boyfriends used him as an excuse to dump me. I read out Subbu's letter. Samir was furious: 'When I meet this bastard, I promise I will kill him.' The steely resolve in his voice had frightened me.

I wonder if Samir has always had it in him to let his sudden bouts of rage take over. Or could he kill even otherwise? Snuff out a life after a few days of quiet deliberation? A fetish that he has kept successfully hidden from the rest of the world?

He always had a cruel streak in him. When we were in high school, one of his girlfriends had once complained to me that Samir had tried to strangle her when she told him she was no longer interested in going out with him. I had watched, fascinated, as she'd unbuttoned her collar and pointed at the bruises on her neck.

The way he dumped his girlfriends after he was through with them had always left me a little rattled. I knew one of them had tried to kill herself after Samir had unceremoniously dumped her. It had happened in Paris and he had called me to boast about it later.

'The stupid cow,' he had gloated. 'She couldn't even manage dying properly. She should have asked me to help her. I would have gladly killed her. You have no idea how irritating she had become in the last few weeks.'

I had hung up on him after sternly admonishing him. I was studying at the management institute in Kolkata those days and learning to view everything from the perspective of logic and reason. Excesses of any kind had no place in my life at that time. And it had always confounded me how Samir could be gentle and sensitive with me on the one hand and behave like such a cad with his girlfriends on the other.

Had I missed out on something obvious all this while? For men, didn't it always go back to the relationship they shared with their mother? Samir and Vrinda have always had a troubled relationship even though she was always trying to be a good mother – driving down from Coimbatore every month when we were in school and bringing him back to the cottage for the weekends. The school rules didn't allow for it but she had managed to convince the principal with a white lie, claiming that her son had a skin ailment that necessitated a visit to a specialist every month. Once Samir and I got into high school and became friends, she managed to get permission for me to accompany them sometimes too. Of course my mother's concurrence had to be sought. She was more than happy to do so. She believed Samir and his mother were good influences and that I would only benefit by being with them.

Vrinda's wealth had something to do with my mother's whole-hearted approval of her and Samir.

Despite everything Vrinda has done for him, Samir has always been angry with his mother. Maybe all boys are like that. I don't think he ever forgave Vrinda for marrying again.

I force myself to think whether his rage against his mother gets transferred to older women with whom he has intimate relations. My mother and he were certainly close.

Vrinda tells me he had also been in touch with Karla for the past six months. 'She had helped a friend of his get a job in her school.'

'What friend?'

'A girl called Sujala. She moved here with her husband a year ago. Samir was painting her portrait.'

'He has never mentioned her to me and it's not like Samir to do portraits.'

'I know. But they talked him into some kind of a commission.'

'When has Samir needed to earn money through his paintings?'

'That you have to ask him. You know he never tells me anything. I thought you would know about her.'

'We haven't been around each other much in the last couple of years. When Ma died I thought he would come to Lucknow for the funeral. But when I called him he said much as he wanted to come he couldn't as had the flu. I felt he was telling a lie but I was in no state of mind to fight with him then.' At that time I had thought it was his inability to handle any kind of crisis that had kept Samir away.

'He didn't tell me about it. In fact, I learnt about your mother's death from him only a few months ago. This last one year Randeep and I have been busy trying to expand our business,' Vrinda says tiredly. 'And for the past three months I thought he had stabilized, ever since that woman...' she looks at me suddenly and trails off.

'Ever since?' I ask her.

'It's not important,' she says, sounding edgy.

The throbbing ache is back in my head.

I was working on a project report before I left Delhi. I go back to the comfort of my laptop to keep away from aggravating thoughts and lose myself in figures and data. I am all alone in the cottage for the night. Vrinda is staying over at the club with her husband. She has asked for food to be delivered to me from there. She calls to tell me the lawyer has been able to organize a bail hearing for Samir with the local magistrate.

'Randeep has taken care of the local authorities. They are not making much of a case against Samir as he was only found at the site of the murder. There is nothing to link him with the crime.'

I know what 'taking care' means when the wealthy use that phrase.

'Your friend is going to be let off soon,' she says cheerfully before hanging up.

When we were in Class IX, I got into trouble with all my classmates. We had a Physics teacher everybody detested. She liked to surprise us with class tests on portions of the curricula that she hadn't taught us. One day the entire class decided they would give in blank answer-sheets the next time she did this to us. Everyone honoured the pact, including Lipika who came first in class. Everyone, except me. I refused to abide by the class decision and instead struggled with the unfamiliar questions and gave in my paper with a few sentences and many more scratches. I knew I would fail the test but that wasn't the point.

The class was furious at my betrayal and decided to stop talking to me. That is the worst possible punishment that can be meted out to a student in boarding school. But Samir chose to rebel. He refused to fall in line with the diktat and asked me why I had behaved so irrationally.

'I knew the class would punish me. What I wasn't sure about was whether you would join them. I had to find out.'

'Why is that important to you?'

'I don't know. But it is.'

'Both of us are such freaks of nature,' I remember Samir telling me that day.

Neither of us needed to say anything to each other after that. For all the time I was boycotted by the rest of the class, Samir was ignored too. For a week, we had only each other for company.

It was the happiest week of my childhood.

Like the brightest star...

Vrinda calls again in the morning to check whether I would like to accompany the rest of them to the court where the magistrate is going to be taking a call on Samir's bail plea. I tell her I have a headache and the drive up and down the winding road will make me sick. She tells me not to worry. 'The hearing is meant to be at noon. By the time they get him back and release him, it will be late evening.'

'Are you sure he is going to be let off?' I ask.

'I am not considering any other possibility. I told you everything has been arranged.' The irritation in her voice is clearly audible as she hangs up.

I make some coffee for myself and go out to the porch with my cup. Samir's red Beetle seems to have been newly painted. I had failed to notice it all the time I have been in the cottage. The antique car has been his most enduring love. He inherited it from his grandfather, Vrinda's dad.

I cannot understand why I am feeling so light despite the revelations of the previous day. My eyes fall on a lavish blue carpet of blooms in a corner of the garden. It is the Kurinji that blossoms once in twelve years. In all my childhood years spent here, I have seen them only once. The teachers had made a big deal about them and brought us in batches to the hills to show us the rare flowers. I walk towards them, mesmerized.

'They are beautiful, aren't they?'

I look up, startled, to find a twinkling pair of eyes peering down at me from the other side of the fence.

She is old. The wrinkles, formed many years ago, have settled comfortably around her eyes and her mouth. The silver white hair on her head is still lush.

'Hello,' I say a little reluctantly. Old folks are not my favourites. Especially women. I feel that they disapprove of me. This one is sizing me up behind all that smiling and nodding. I am sure of it.

'What are they saying about Samir? I hope they are going to release him soon.'

'Erm… I guess so.' I am not so sure I want to continue with this conversation.

'It is we women who are responsible for the downfall of good men,' she says dropping her voice and bringing her face close to mine.

I draw back unconsciously. But she is determined to have her say. 'He was the nicest young man until she came to live with him… I told my friends she is going to destroy him. Moving in with him like that just because her husband had to go back for a few months.'

'Who was living with Samir?' I have always been interested in Samir's girlfriends. Not interested in a jealous kind of a way, but more in a 'what is this one all about' way.

The old woman is suddenly wary. Maybe she realizes she has blurted out more than she intended to. 'I am sorry… I have to go. I was cooking when I saw you in the garden. I just came out to enquire about Samir.'

'They should release him today. That's what his mother says,' I tell her with a smile. I want her to stay and tell me more about this woman who was living with Samir.

'That's good to know,' she says and disappears.

I bend over the Kurinji once again, marvelling at their unique purplish-blue. My eyes fall on a tiny glittering object lying on the ground next to one of the shrubs. It is an ear stud, a tiny diamond aflash on a sliver of gold. It is partly covered in mud. I pick it up and rub it against my shirt to clean it. I am sure of one thing now.

The woman who was living with Samir had good taste in jewellery.

By the time Samir and Vrinda come home it is almost eight. I have spent most of the day sleeping. It is really strange. Everything I have heard after coming to Coonoor should have had me on edge. But here I have to just stretch and my eyes start to droop. I wonder whether the habit is a throwback to the days when I was growing up. When Samir and I came to spend weekends with Vrinda we used to sleep a lot. The cottage was our sleep retreat. The strict regimen in the hostel required us to be up at dawn. So we would do our best to catch up while we could. Some habits are difficult to get rid of.

You can say that about relationships too.

Samir goes to the bathroom to shave and shower while Vrinda makes coffee for the both of us. She comes to my room with two steaming mugs.

'I want you to stay here for a few days with Samir. Please find out from him how he got into this mess.'

'I have to get back to Delhi soon or I will lose my job,' is my lame rejoinder to her request, that could very well be an order.

'You can always get another job.' She hesitates; I know there is something she wants to add but is nervous I might get offended.

'I work because I want to. Ma left me a lot of money as well as the house in Lucknow.' It is my turn to pre-empt her.

'I am sorry. You have to understand this hasn't been easy for me. After they arrested Samir all I could think about was getting him out. When it was over today and we were driving down to the cottage, I thought of Karla. She was one of my closest friends. We had the kind of friendship Samir and you have. I had helped her get this job and feel responsible in some way for her death. And I haven't had the luxury of grieving for her as yet.'

I wonder whether I should tell her that I too have things to grieve about.

Maybe more than she knows about.

Maybe more than even I know about.

Samir walks in just then and both of us stare at him in silence. He is looking more like himself. Although I have known him for years, I have never quite got used to how good looking he is. One of the girls in the school, hopelessly in love with Samir and jealous of our relationship, had nicknamed us 'Beauty and the Beast'. When Samir found out, he couldn't stop teasing me about being labelled the beast. I never told him that I had cried that night. I have always kept some things from him. Now I am learning he has been doing the same.

Vrinda says she will get him some coffee and goes into the kitchen.

'It is just like old times, don't you think?' Samir says pulling the large bean bag next to my bed.

'No. It is not!' I am aware my voice is sounding sharper than I intended it to be.

He stares at me, looking confused, and then realization dawns in his eyes. 'I am sorry, Neha. I know I should have told you about being in Lucknow when Ratna was killed. But I promise you I had nothing to do with it.'

When we were young Samir used to address my mother as Aunty. The formality was dispensed with once we grew up.

'You made a trip to Lucknow and didn't tell me about it? Why did Ma keep it away from me?'

'Because I asked her to.'

I am so angry that I find it difficult to find the words to condemn both of them.

'I will explain everything, Neha. Just give me some time, okay? And for now please don't mention the similarities in the circumstances of both the deaths. Especially to Mum.'

'Coffee is ready,' Vrinda says brightly, coming into the room. Samir gets up to take his mug from the tray and says he will have it in his room. Vrinda follows him after imploring me to eat before I sleep. Mother and son have eaten in the club on their way to the cottage and have brought me a packed meal. After a few minutes I hear a car revving up. It is clear Samir has managed to fob off his mother. Vrinda has gone back to the club to be with her husband, leaving behind the two of us.

The cottage feels very cold all of a sudden.

On not so clear nights

I have no idea what time I fell asleep the previous night. After Vrinda left, I thought Samir would come to my room to resume our conversation. He didn't. As for me, I sat in my room, immobilized. I knew I had to do something to understand what was happening to me, what was becoming of my life. But I just couldn't.

The last time I had met Mother we had fought. I was still smarting from Subbu's betrayal and needed someone to blame. I had read an article in a magazine I had picked up from an airport bookstore that children from broken families had trouble holding on to relationships when they grew up. My family history was different. For all practical purposes, I had a father and a mother. Except, the man didn't want to acknowledge me. That qualified me to be a part of this exclusive club. As if on cue my mother had called the same evening. She had insisted that I come to Lucknow for the weekend. She had seemed unnaturally preoccupied when she'd come to pick me up from the airport.

The next morning she had asked me to accompany her to her bank so that she could convert all her individual accounts into a joint one with me. She was an officer in the Revenue department and when I learnt what her savings amounted to, I had baulked. There was no way she could have saved so much on her own salary. Even if she was putting all of it in the bank and the man paid for everything else including the house we called our own and my expensive education. First the boarding school, then the graduation in Economics followed by an MBA, all in elite institutions. I was too embarrassed to create a scene in the presence of the oily bank manager and quietly signed the documents he put forth.

But I had let her have it once we got back home.

'I don't need his filthy money!' I screamed.

'Don't talk about him like that.' She had been angry as well.

'I don't want to talk about him at all. I don't want anything to do with him.'

'You don't understand anything.'

'What is there to understand? For him I am nothing more than a dispensable piece of garbage he has spawned. I am sure there are many more in this world. After all, you can't be the only mistress he has, what with all his power and influence.'

'How dare you talk to me like that!'

'Why? Does the truth hurt?'

'I thought you had grown up. In fact, this time I wanted to tell you everything.'

'Save yourself the trouble. I have no interest in the sordid details of your disgusting affair.'

'I am warning you.'

'I am leaving. All I want you to do is to tell him that he needn't try to bribe me. I am not proud of having him as my father, in case he is under that mistaken notion. Tell him, even if he doesn't pay me, I won't tell the world about our relationship. And please leave me alone, the both of you.'

'Listen there is something you must know…'

But I ran out, only dimly registering that her words were veiled in tears. I stormed out of the house with just my handbag, took a cab to the airport, and flew back the same evening to Delhi, messaging her only after reaching my flat.

She had texted back saying, 'We will talk when you are less angry. You will understand everything then.'

The next time I saw her she was dead.

I can't stop thinking about Samir and Mother. What else have they been hiding from me? Why were they meeting each other without my knowledge? Why had Samir gone to Lucknow around the time of her death?

I feel like going to Samir's room and shaking him. It is high time he told me what is going on.

I stand near his door for a long time. He is snoring so loudly that I can hear him from outside. I don't know why but I change my mind about waking him up.

Maybe I know I don't have the strength to listen to his answers in the dead of night.

He is not in the cottage when I wake up. Neither is his red Beetle. I make myself a cup of coffee and for the first time since I have been in the cottage, make my way to the stairs that lead to the large studio. Samir is not there either but my attention is riveted by a large portrait of a beautiful woman that stands out among the landscapes he normally paints. It is a nude. She is sprawled on a long easy chair, next to a small table with a vase that holds a bunch of Kurinji blossoms. Her mouth has the contours of one who is in two minds about smiling at the world. The kind of look you have when you run into someone you think you recognize but you can't be sure. She could be in her late twenties, or younger. It's difficult to tell.

I have known most of Samir's girlfriends and this one does not conform to type. There is an air of intrigue about her, as if life has revealed many secrets that she is unwilling to share. I draw closer to the portrait. Although only one of her ears is visible because of the way she is reclining, I am sure I recognize the stud I found in the garden.

An irrational guilt takes over.

As if I have committed a crime by picking up something that belongs to her.

I am unable to hold her gaze and turn away. My eyes fall on something concealed behind the portraits in one corner. It is a thick coil of rope. I haven't seen either of the corpses and don't know whether a similar rope was used to bind the hands of the victims, and yet the sight of it frightens me. I turn away in a daze and run blindly down the stairs. As I sit down on my bed trying to get back my breath, I wonder what has made me so nervous.

Was it the portrait or that coil of rope sitting there like a fat python?

Vrinda comes over at eleven and is distressed to find that her son is not home. 'Why did you let him go?' she asks me. The hint of accusation in her voice is not hard to discern.

'He left before I woke up.'

She looks at me silently, her body language communicating her disapproval. Maybe it is my state of mind after coming across the portrait in the studio but I get angry because it is evident she is blaming me for Samir disappearing like this, early in the morning. I am unable to contain myself. 'Your friend and my mother were killed in the same manner.'

'*What?* What are you saying?' She looks shocked.

'My mother was hit on the head with a blunt object and then the killer bludgeoned her face to pulp. After she died the murderer folded her hands and tied them together, making it look as if she was pleading for mercy. She was drugged before the murderer attacked her. That's what the police told me.'

The shock on Vrinda's face makes me ashamed about the abrupt way I have broken the news to her.

She sits down heavily on a chair and looks away. An uncomfortable silence takes over.

'Have you told this to anyone else?' she finally manages to ask.

'No.'

'What about Samir?'

'He told me last night that he was in Lucknow when she was killed.'

'I am sure there is a misunderstanding. He doted on your mother.'

'That's what I used to think too.'

35

She is battling unsuccessfully to find words to articulate her confusion. But something about the distress writ large on her face eggs me on to continue relentlessly. 'I guess that's what he meant when I met him in the lock-up; remember he told me that he didn't have anything to do with *either* of them?' I say.

'Krishnamachari asked him about that after he was released. But he denied saying anything like that to you. He said you didn't understand what he was trying to say,' Vrinda blurts out angrily.

I shrug knowing that single action of mine is more eloquent than anything I can put in words. I wonder whether I should tell her about the coil of rope in the studio upstairs. I decide against it.

I am no longer sure whether I can trust her anymore.

She leaves after some time. After composing herself enough to tell me I should not jump to conclusions and that Samir is likely to have a very good explanation about everything.

'I am banking on the same,' I tell her dryly.

'Listen, please ask him to call me as soon as he gets back. The lawyer needs to talk to him some more to prepare his case and he better tell him everything.'

She hesitates a bit before adding, 'Even that bit about being in Lucknow when your mother met with her unfortunate accident.'

'It wasn't an accident. She was murdered.'

She ignores the last sentence as she gets into the car and drives away.

I suddenly discover how hungry I am and go into the kitchen to fix myself some toast and eggs.

It is late afternoon and Samir isn't back. Vrinda has called twice enquiring about him. I have had enough of sitting cooped up in the cottage and am seriously wondering whether it is a good idea on my part to go on staying with someone who may be responsible for the murder of my mother. The whole thing is a bit surreal.

But deep down I find it difficult to believe that Samir could have had anything to do with Mother's murder. There is comfort in the thought that someone is trying to frame Samir for the two murders.

It is funny how the mind works when you want to protect someone you love. I have discovered it isn't as if I didn't care for my mother. But I seem to have reclaimed my love for her only after I came to Coonoor and started to uncover certain facts about her murder. I have also simultaneously discovered in the last two days that my love for my mother is not powerful enough for me to have the strength to condemn Samir. I try to convince myself that's how Mother would have wanted it. She was so fond of Samir that she could let him get away with anything. Even murder.

The conflict I have in my head about Samir is going to continue until he confesses to the reason behind him meeting Mother without my knowledge. And even then, if I figure out he is lying about something, I don't know whether my first impulse will be to inform the authorities, or to protect him.

I tell myself I should check into a hotel. Staying on in this place is not going to help me have an objective perspective. Suddenly I find it unbearable inside the cottage. I decide to get out of the house and get some fresh air.

It is chilly and the windcheater I have borrowed from the coat cupboard next to the front door, apart from being oversized, is inadequate to keep the cold away. I push my hands resolutely inside the pockets and begin a brisk walk but my teeth continue to chatter. I consider turning back when my eyes fall on a signboard that says 'Sunshine Departmental Store.'

I don't remember seeing the shop when I used to come and stay in Samir's cottage during our school days. It is too small for what it claims to be but what it lacks in size, it makes up in warmth – generated by a room heater. There is just one shopper being served by a young salesgirl. A middle-aged man sits behind the counter, his eyes riveted to a small television set placed diagonally opposite him on an elevated shelf. A cricket match is on and he looks away from the screen to smile briefly at me, revealing brittle, tobacco-stained teeth. The shopper, an old woman in trousers and an oversized sweater, looks keenly at me as she shuffles towards the counter with the salesgirl behind her carrying a couple of small, brown, paper bags.

I notice three or four white plastic tables with blue plastic chairs around them in the middle of the store. My eyes fall on an Espresso machine with paper cups beside it. There is also a glass counter displaying tempting pastries and sandwiches next to the machine.

I go and sit on one of the chairs. The salesgirl comes bustling over to me. 'What can I get you?'

'A cup of coffee, please. What are the sandwiches you have?'

'Cheese and chicken.'

'I'll have the chicken.'

'Can I get you a brownie as well? They are our speciality.'

'Please.'

I am ravenous. Maybe it is the cold combined with all the walking I have done but as soon as the sandwich arrives I demolish it and then get to work on the brownie that follows. When the girl comes back with the Espresso I tell her I would like to have a cheese sandwich too. She nods her head and turns to go.

'Also another brownie.' I have been pecking at the food Vrinda has been sending from the club for the last two days; the deprivation is finally beginning to tell.

I have my back to the entrance and yet I am aware there is no one apart from the three of us in the place. Suddenly I hear the door creak and a pleasant voice call out, 'Good evening' in what sounds like an American accent. I turn to look. The new customer looks Indian despite the accent but I cannot see him clearly. He is talking to the man at the counter with his back to me. Suddenly the man at the counter calls out, startling me into spilling a bit of my Espresso on the windcheater. 'Can you come here for a minute, Harini? Mr Dayal wants to know whether a friend of his visited the store today. I have told him I was here most of the day except for the two hours I take for lunch.'

'Is he asking about the young man who stayed with them last year?' Harini says, walking towards me with the cheese sandwich and the brownie; she wants to finish serving me first.

'Yeah... was he here?' It is that pleasant American voice again.

This time I catch a good glimpse of him when I turn. He is in his late thirties. Tall and well built with round-rimmed spectacles that, if anything, add to the charm of his intelligent face. There is something attractive about this man, especially in the way he carries himself. You can be at ease in his presence because of the solidity he carries. He looks like a grown-up Harry Potter. He stares at me for a second before his attention is drawn to Harini. Long enough to tell me his eyes carry all the stress he is feeling at that moment.

'Well,' says Harini slowly, as if she needs time to think. 'Mr Dayal is the second person to have asked about him today. As soon as I opened the store today, just before you came in, the artist was here enquiring about him too.'

'Who? Are you talking about Samir?' The man with the American accent moves closer to my table to question the girl. I can feel his presence behind me.

'Yes, I told him the same thing. That your friend from America didn't come to the store.'

'You would recognize him, won't you, if he came here?'

'Yes, I remember him from last year. There is no way I can forget that face.'

I know I have to say something now or it will be too late. 'Has Samir been here, then?'

I find three pairs of baffled eyes coming to rest on me.

'This has nothing to do with Samir,' the man frowns and abruptly leaves the store.

Who knows better than a sinner?

The hills are always in a hurry to embrace the dark. The sun, which has been an occasional visitor through the day, has disappeared completely when I come out of the store. My head is in a whirl. Why did the man with the American accent rush out of the store like that when I asked about Samir? Why had he and Samir come to the store to enquire about the same person?

The lights in the cottage and the Beetle parked in the porch inform me that Samir is back. I am determined to get all my answers tonight. There is no way I am going to allow him to get away this time, regardless of any fresh set of excuses he may come up with. I decide I am going to confront him, come what may, and make it so difficult for him that he can't but respond.

The angry man who answers the doorbell is in no mood to be conciliatory. He pulls me inside and stands looking at me, shaking with rage. I have never seen Samir this angry.

'Let go of me. You are hurting me,' I splutter, pushing him away.

'Why did you tell her?'

'Tell her what?'

'You know what I am talking about. I told you specifically not to tell Mum about the two murders being similarly executed.'

'One of the victims was my mother, in case you don't remember,' I say and burst into tears. All the tension I have been bottling up comes out and I am unable to stop the sobbing, however hard I try.

'Shit... I am so sorry, Neha,' Samir says gathering me in his arms. Very soon he is crying too. We are back in school. I may as well be telling him that my life sucks and he is responding in kind to indicate things are not much better with his life either.

After what seems like an eternity, I calm myself enough to release myself from Samir's embrace. 'You should tell me everything. I have had enough of this shadow chasing.'

'I can tell you a part of it. But not everything. For that you will have to be patient.'

'At least tell me what was going on between Ma and you?'

'I had asked Ratna for some help. She was trying to locate someone for me.'

'Locate who?'

'This woman I got to know when I started living here after returning from Paris. I was in love with her and then she disappeared for a while. Ratna was the only one I could turn to. Because of her political contacts.'

'The girl whose portrait you have painted?'

'How do you know about that?'

'Your neighbour mentioned her to me and Vrinda Aunty also spoke about her. I saw the nude this morning.'

'I bet Mum pumped you up with all this information and then got exactly what she wanted out of you.'

'That's not fair. I told her about Ma's death because I was angry with you for disappearing this morning.'

'You are so immature, Neha. Please understand, I can't trust Mum with anything and I can't reveal anything till the murderer is found. Especially Ratna's murderer. Linking the two deaths is just going to complicate matters for me and help the person who is trying to frame me.'

'But why are the murders similar? And how come you are linked to both?'

'That's the idea, don't you see? To implicate me for both of them.'

'Who would want to do that?'

'That's what I am trying to find out.'

The whole argument between us sounds facetious to my ears. It is like we are back in school and Samir is once again defending his reasons for callously dumping his latest girlfriend. 'You have to explain everything properly to me. This is no good.'

'I will, I promise you. Just give me another day. I have to go out now. If Mum calls, tell her I am in my room sleeping. I will speak to her tomorrow morning.'

'Don't run off like that.'

He pauses near the front door to look at me. 'What's it now? I told you I am in a hurry,' the irritation is back in his voice.

'When are you going to be back?'

'As soon as possible. If I am not home in a couple of hours, go to bed. I promise that by tomorrow you will know everything I know.'

And he leaves the house once again.

Vrinda does not call. Instead she comes over. On the pretext of getting dinner for the two of us. She is angry once again on not finding the car in the porch. She demands to know from me where her son is. I tell her I am sick of being caught between the two of them and that if either of them uses me again I will just check into a hotel. She has the grace to look embarrassed. She asks me whether I am hungry. I tell her I ate an hour ago. I want her to leave. If Samir comes back and finds his mother at home, he is bound to clam up again.

But Vrinda is determined to prise out all the information from her son. She says I can go to bed if I want and she will wait for Samir to come back. I give up and go to my room.

I am woken up in the middle of the night by an agitated Vrinda. She has got a call from a hospital. Samir has been in an accident. The injuries are serious.

Samir is in the ICU and the doctor tells us he is yet to regain consciousness. They are doing their best but the accident was bad. The doctors and the nurses are being infuriatingly evasive. His stepfather arrives from the club a few minutes after us and I look away as he takes a sobbing Vrinda in his arms. I can't stop myself from feeling guilty. I should have stopped Samir. Not that he would have listened. He is stubborn as a mule. Once he decides on a course of action, it is impossible to stop him from doing what he wants.

After I have recovered from the initial shock, the uncomfortable thought occurs to me that it may not have been an accident at all. The same person who murdered my mother and Vrinda's friend may have decided to do away with Samir as well. After all, Samir had mentioned that someone was trying to frame him.

It had taken me many years to find out I was different from the other children with whom I went to school; they could lay claim to their parents in a way I never could. Around the same time I had started to develop a fear of confined spaces. Whenever I got into a lift and the doors closed I felt the walls were closing in on me.

Waiting outside the ICU along with Vrinda and Randeep feels just as claustrophobic. I am struggling to breathe while the same thought runs again and again through my head.

'Dear God, please don't let him die.'

They tell us early the next morning that Samir has slipped into a coma and it is difficult to say when he will regain consciousness. Vrinda wants to know whether he has suffered permanent damage to the brain. The doctors are not sure. All they can tell us is that we should wait and pray that Samir recovers fast.

They also ask us to go home and rest for a while.

I am a child once again and home for the holidays. I am sleeping with Mother next to me. Suddenly the door creaks open and the man enters. I am awake now but I don't want him to find out. I try to lie as still as I can and watch him through half-opened eyes. He sits by her side looking straight ahead. Suddenly he turns towards Mother and wraps his fingers around her throat. Samir slips silently into the room. I have no recall of what Samir looked like when he was seven. He is the grown up Samir and he is sneering.

Mother thrashes her arms and legs and then lies still. Lying next to her, almost unable to breathe, I reach out tentatively and touch one of her palms. It feels very cold. The man gets up slowly and stands watching while Samir takes out a rope, folds her hands and ties them together. The man comes closer and pats him on the back. They leave the room together, pausing near the door to throw a last look at the two of us.

The dream is so vivid that I wake up sweating.

I must have fallen asleep after Vrinda and Randeep dropped me back to the cottage on their way to the club. I sit up and look blankly all around. The space feels alien. As if I have no right to be there. I tell myself I need to get out of here fast.

I go to the kitchen to make some coffee. The clock tells me it is eleven in the morning. We had left the hospital in the early hours of dawn. Vrinda dropped me off at the gate after a distracted, 'I will see you in the day as soon as I can. Maybe it is a good idea for you to shift in to the club with us.'

The doorbell rings suddenly breaking my chain of thought. I trudge slowly to the door expecting it to be either Vrinda or the boy who gets me my meals from the club.

It is the woman from the painting.

She is beautiful; almost ethereally so. She stands near the door wearing a lavender coloured shirt over blue jeans with a grey shawl thrown carelessly about her shoulders – her only concession to the windy morning. She has pale almost translucent skin and wide soft brown eyes. Her nose is sharp and pinched and the full lips that follow curl in a smile of recognition before my startled eyes.

'Hi...You must be Neha. I am Sujala... Aren't you going to ask me in?'

'Hello, please come in,' I say uncertainly.

'You must be wondering how I know your name,' she says tossing her shawl on a chair and sitting down on another. 'Samir always talked such a lot about you. And I have also seen your pictures in his school album.'

'Samir has been in an accident,' I tell her. 'He is in the ICU.'

It is her turn to be startled. 'When did this happen?' There is a catch in her voice. It could be shock. It could also be pretence. I sense that with her it is always going to be difficult to tell.

'Last night.'

'What time?'

'I don't know. It was around seven when he left the cottage.'

'Do you have any idea who he was going to meet?'

She has caught me by surprise. It occurs to me that I am not under any obligation to provide her with information. Samir didn't say much about her to me even when I asked about her portrait. I have no knowledge about the current status of their relationship. I think it best to shrug my shoulders in response.

'You have to forgive me. I am a friend of Samir's. In fact, I lived with him in this cottage for a few months,'

47

she offers slowly, all the while looking at me. Maybe I am making her uncertain too.

'I saw your portrait...'

'That's how our friendship began. My husband asked Samir to paint me. Of course, that wasn't the painting you saw,' she blushes and looks away. 'With all this police business, I would much rather take the portrait back with me.'

'Does your husband know Samir has painted you in the nude?' I can't resist asking.

She shrugs impatiently. 'Yeah, he knows. I am not worried about that. It's just that I don't want any unnecessary complications in my life right now. Because of the portrait and because I knew Karla, the cops could decide to harass me. In fact, my husband suggested I ask Samir for the painting,' she concludes wearily. She is sounding out of breath, her words running over each other.

'Would you like a glass of water?' I don't know why but I don't want her to leave.

'No, thank you. I will help myself,' she pauses once again and then looks directly into my eyes: 'I think he saw you in the store last evening.'

'Who did?'

'My husband, Kabir.'

The doorbell rings and I get up to open the door. Vrinda comes in. 'I have been to the hospital. Samir is still unconscious,' she starts to tell me before her shocked eyes fall on the visitor.

'Hi Vrinda, I am so sorry to hear about Samir's accident,' Sujala says, getting up to greet her.

'What are you doing here?' is Vrinda's frosty response.

You can slice the tension in the room with a knife. It is evident that Vrinda hates this woman. It is difficult to know what Sujala thinks of Vrinda. But then, I think, it would be difficult to gauge what Sujala thinks about anyone. After a few minutes of uneasy silence, she gets up and says she is leaving and would like to visit Samir in the hospital.

'He is in the ICU. They don't encourage visitors,' the curtness with which Vrinda makes her statement startles me.

I am reminded of something after Sujala has gone out of the front door and is near the gate. 'Hey… wait!' I call out.

She pauses to look back at me.

'I think I have something that belongs to you.'

She frowns in confusion.

'Give me a second, will you?' I say and go to my room to fetch her ear-stud.

It is there glinting on the bedside table. I pick it up and go back to the living room. Vrinda is standing near the door with a half quizzical look on her face. She hasn't asked Sujala to come back inside to wait.

I give her the earring.

'Wow, where did you find it? I have been looking for it for months now,' she smiles.

'Found it near the Kurinji shrubs yesterday.'

She turns to go. Suddenly she stops and turns towards me once again.

'How did you know it belongs to me?'

'From the portrait.'

'I guess I will have to come back for that later.'

'Yes,' I agree. 'You will have to wait for Samir. I can't give away any of his paintings in his absence. But you could ask Vrinda?'

'You think Vrinda would let me touch any of her son's precious belongings?'

'But it is your painting.'

'Try telling her that... don't worry, I will come back when Samir gets home and claim what is rightfully mine,' she says half in jest and leaves. I stand near the gate watching her disappear down the end of the road, until an impatient Vrinda calls out for me from inside.

Reluctant hosts

Vrinda has a new trick up her sleeve. She wants me to go back to Delhi. I am furious when I hear her say this. She tells me that even Randeep feels that there is not much point in my staying on. They have decided to shift Samir to a hospital in Coimbatore as soon as the doctors will allow it. He has a broken kneecap in addition to injuries on the head and the medical facilities in Coimbatore are much better.

What she leaves out is that her family owns half the city. They have textile mills, factories producing automotive spare parts, computer-training institutes, hospitals, software organizations, schools and an engineering college named after her grandfather. All of which belong to Vrinda now. She had a brother who was a manic-depressive. He had killed himself a few years ago. Samir had been devastated. He was very fond of his uncle and blamed Vrinda for the suicide. At the time, I had thought he was being unfair.

'She never let him forget how much more efficient she was. The inadequacy gnawed at him until he couldn't live with it any longer.'

'You tend to blame her for anything that goes wrong in your life,' I remember saying to him.

'She is not your mother. How would you know?'

I am learning now that there was some merit to the poison Samir habitually spewed about his mother. He has most likely inherited her capacity to use and discard people; to get them out of the way when they turn into inconveniences. I wonder whether Vrinda will stop at anything to get rid of me if she believed I could jeopardize Samir's case.

The man she is married to appears to be as ruthless as her. Randeep hails from an equally affluent family. They own tea and coffee estates all around the Ooty–Coonoor belt. He is charming as hell, always getting up if a woman enters the room, but behind the genteel facade I have always sensed a tension. His eyes dart about as if trying to peep into all the nooks and corners that others miss. They make a formidable duo, Vrinda and him.

'Don't be fooled by how suave he appears,' Samir had shared with me, a day after his mother got married again. We were having tea in the garden of his palatial house in Coimbatore.

I had been telling him how charming I found his new stepfather. I had teased him saying he was jealous because all his girlfriends were likely to fall for him.

'No, seriously,' Samir had insisted. 'Last week, both of us went shopping for golf clubs. On our way back, we stopped near a traffic signal and a street urchin came and started tapping at his window. I could see he was getting annoyed. He rolled down his window and I thought he was going to give the kid a tenner. That's what Ma usually does. But as soon as the poor wretch stretched her hands inside, Randeep started rolling up the window again. She would have lost her hand if she hadn't pulled it out in time! There was something in his face at that time. Like he would have enjoyed it if she had lost her hand. It completely spooked me.'

'What a story. I am sure you are making it up,' I had chided him, laughing.

The rich are always incestuous. They mate only with their own. And in Randeep's and Vrinda's case, I realize, they are similar in more ways than one. Both of them can be brutally self-serving when it suits them. I am sure their business adversaries have a healthy respect for them. From what I have learnt from Samir, they are fiercely competitive and have tried their best to get Samir interested in the business. He has steadfastly stayed away, preferring to stay and paint in the cottage that Vrinda had bought as a weekend retreat when Samir was admitted to boarding school.

Vrinda can get the best doctors in Coimbatore to wait hand and foot on her son. So it makes sense in one way. What I can't understand is how she has ruled out the possibility that her son may regain consciousness before he is shifted to Coimbatore. In which case, shouldn't I be around to ferret out the information for which I have been summoned all the way from Delhi?

Not surprisingly, just as I am working out all these things in my head, Vrinda has intuited my thoughts. 'We plan to shift him tomorrow. You can stay on until then. But you have to shift to the club with us tonight. It is not safe for you to go on staying here after what has happened to Samir.'

'Why don't you shift to the cottage instead?' I ask her.

'It is more convenient at the club. I find it easier to work from there. With neither of us being in Coimbatore, I am afraid work is just piling up.'

I am surprised she has taken the trouble to drive down all the way to the cottage just to relay this message. Vrinda could have easily called me on the phone. There is an agenda behind her personally coming over. My suspicions are not unfounded. The brakes of Samir's car were tampered with. Vrinda says the police have started their investigations and as someone who was staying with Samir when he left the house, they want me to give a statement. She wants to personally escort me to the police station.

'It will be easier this way. With me around, they won't be able to bully you,' she says.

Once again she makes it sound as if she is doing me a favour by going out of her way to accompany me to meet the cops. Although the real reason behind her magnanimous act, I suspect, is to ensure that I don't give out any information to the cops that could further jeopardize Samir's case. Like the similarities in the murders of Mother and Karla.

The police station looks small and damp on the outside. The path that leads to it is slushy. A couple of men in khaki uniforms lurk around outside, smoking. They look at us with narrowed eyes as we get off the car. They must be trying to figure out what two women in a luxury car driven by a uniformed chauffeur are doing in a place that usually entertains petty criminals.

There is a small man sitting behind a table. He gets up as soon as he sees Vrinda. She speaks in Tamil to him. My own grip on the language is tenuous despite having lived and studied in these parts for many years. Back in school, the teachers punished us if we spoke to each other in a language other than English. However I do understand that what she is asking the man is to hurry with the proceedings. He nods subserviently. She has obviously got someone higher up in the ranks to speak to the station in-charge. He is behaving more like Vrinda's personal retainer.

He turns to me and asks me something in Tamil. Vrinda looks at me while I grapple with a response. 'Please speak in English,' she says impatiently. 'Isn't that our official language?' The challenge in her voice is unmistakable.

'Sorry, Madam,' the man looks sheepish. Wealth and influence are enough to silence the law-keepers. If Samir had had anything to do with Mother's death, all that would be required of Vrinda to convince the cops he was innocent would be to land up and flaunt her affluence. I tell myself I am being too cynical. If Vrinda's influence really was so all-pervasive, Samir would not have spent two days in police custody.

The station in-charge asks me to write down the events leading to Samir's leaving the cottage last night and driving away. He says I should put in the name of the person he was going to meet. He looks disappointed when I tell him Samir did not tell me this. He wants to know next why I was staying in the cottage and if the two of us are related. When I say I am Samir's friend, he gives me a mocking half-smile. Vrinda looks at him sternly, 'They have been together since school,' she says, as if that piece of information would stop the sneering man from thinking Samir and I are lovers.

I pen down the happenings of the previous day, sticking to the bare outlines and omitting the discussion Samir and I had before he left the cottage. If I bring that in, I would have to reveal the link between my mother's death in faraway Lucknow and Karla's murder. Vrinda takes the paper from me as soon as I finish writing and her eyes scan it quickly. The station in-charge is looking at both of us.

'Here,' says Vrinda, reverting to Tamil and thrusting the paper at the officer. 'Can we leave now?'

He nods his head and buries himself in the piece of paper as if it contains all the wisdom in the world. He doesn't look up when I turn near the door to thank him.

'That was very decent of you,' Vrinda says to me as soon as we are seated in the car.

'What are you talking about?'

She is silent for some time before she says, 'You have been incredibly supportive. I don't know if I would have been able to deal with the information you have about your mother's death and the fact that Samir might be linked with it.'

'Something tells me he is being framed; though I don't know who would do such a thing,' I force myself to say.

'I knew he was going to get into trouble when he started seeing that woman,' Vrinda says. 'There is something very wrong about that couple. And he got into a brawl with this man who had come to stay with them.'

'Whom are you talking about?'

'That woman and her husband, Kabir. Samir started painting her portrait and for a time was very close to both of them. Then this other man and woman came down looking for them. I understand they were a couple.'

'Searching for whom?' I am sure there is something of importance being said here but I cannot quite put my finger on it.

'That woman who came to the house this morning and her husband,' Vrinda explains patiently. 'I don't think Samir even knew the couple who came to visit them. Apparently, they were all having dinner together and the man suddenly attacked Samir. He was admitted to the same hospital a year back. We were out of the country on business and I had to fly back to be with Samir.'

'Did he tell you about it?'

'Who? Samir? You know him. He never tells me anything. Said it was an accident.'

'Then how did you find out all this?' I know I am asking a rhetorical question. Vrinda always makes it a point to find out what is happening in her son's life. Something that he has always hated about his mother.

'Mrs Sridhar who lives in the cottage next to Sujala and Kabir told Mrs Kashyap. She told me.'

I realize this place is not as sleepy as it appears. There is a robust grapevine manned by prying old ladies who have settled down in the small hill-town. I must make some investigations of my own. I am aware Vrinda is looking at me from the corner of her eye. I stare ahead blankly. I don't want her to start guessing my thoughts again.

Vrinda drops me off at the cottage. She says she will be back in the evening to take me to the hospital. 'Keep your bags packed. You are moving to the club tonight. I will also book your air ticket to Delhi.'

'Please don't bother,' I tell her. 'I will get it done myself when I think it's time to go.'

'I told you, there is no point in you staying on here,' she grumbles as the driver reverses the car. I wait for the car to drive away and turn to the gate. My eyes fall on the window of the cottage next door. A sudden movement behind the curtains tells me someone is out there. I decide now is as good a time as any to find out about Samir's life this last one year, when so many things seem to have happened to him – from a love affair with a married woman to being attacked by a stranger. There has to be some kind of a method in all this madness and who better to tap for information than the old nosy neighbour.

I knock gently on the door even though I can see there is a doorbell. The front gate had creaked loudly when I opened it and the person behind the curtain must certainly have heard it. I hear footsteps approach the door.

The twinkling eyes under a mass of silver hair appraise me. I ask her whether I can have a word. She nods.

The inside of her house contrasts vividly with Samir's. While the cottage I have been staying in hankers for a woman's touch, this one is all pink and purple with tiny dolls arranged in a row on the mantelpiece. As if to complete the image, my eyes fall on knitting needles and a child-sized sweater that's almost finished.

'This is for my grandson who lives in UK,' she says following my eyes. Then she giggles suddenly, 'You may find it hard to believe, but I have had a full life with marriage and kids.'

'I am sorry?' I say, turning to her in my confusion.

'I am sure you thought of me as a spinster. The prying sort who can't stop gloating because a handsome young man she has as a neighbour had been arrested for murder and on being released, conveniently gets into an accident that could have proved fatal for him.'

'You know about that?'

'The tourists have spoilt a lot of things, but this place is still not so big that we cannot find out what is happening to our neighbours. Especially in upper Coonoor. You must have noticed most of the houses are locked here. That's because most of the old residents have turned traitors and sold their ancestral homes to rich folk in Madras and Bangalore to be used as holiday homes. But some of us gallantly battle on despite the temptation.'

The locals make a distinction between upper and lower Coonoor. The ones who stay on the climb are affluent and English-speaking. The winding lanes with picturesque cottages could very well be a slice of the Raj. The lower part around the marketplace is for the labourers who work in the estates and petty shop owners. Kipling may very well have had this reference in mind when he made that famous statement about the twain not meeting.

I tell her she reminds me of Mrs Daniel, the Anglo-Indian English teacher we had in school. She smiles and tells me her name is Vidya Kashyap. She lost her husband more than a decade ago to chronic renal failure and stuck on although her daughter didn't like the idea of her staying on her own. Having satisfied herself that she has shared enough information about herself, she starts on me.

Name?

Neha Thakur.

Parents?

I lie to her saying both my parents are dead.

Any siblings?

None.

Am I the same girl who Vrinda used to bring with Samir for weekend stays some years ago?

I learn she didn't always stay in the cottage back then. Her husband was in the Indian Air Force and they were posted to different places but there was the odd occasion when their visits to the cottage coincided with the trips Samir and I made.

Yes. Although I have no recall of seeing or meeting her then, it is possible that on Vrinda's prodding both Samir and I may have greeted her when we ran into her while coming out or going into the cottage, but adolescents don't store such trivia in their memory.

Then she asks me the question that I have asked myself numerous times. Am I in love with Samir?

I am surprised to hear myself saying, I don't know. She smiles and nods absently. Fortified with the lightness I feel at that moment, I start quizzing her about everything she knows about Samir and the woman he painted in the past year.

All about them...

They came down from one of the Mid-western states but nobody had any idea which one. The couple initially stayed in the hotel next to the church. They were plain lucky to get the cottage they bought. Mrs Dastur owned it previously. She had been hale and hearty until a month before the visitors came to Coonoor. She lived in the cottage with a trusted maid who looked after her as well the house. Her children were in the US and visited her once a year.

The decline that set in was abrupt. One day the old lady was spotted taking her usual evening walk accompanied by her maid. And when she woke up the next morning, she had regressed to a state where she was a young newly-married bride and couldn't figure out where she was. The maid said afterwards she had noticed her mistress had been forgetful, but she hadn't realized that things were so bad. Her two sons were summoned from the US and they took her away with them, putting the cottage up for distress sale. Since Kabir and Sujala were also from the US, the children found it easy to relate to them and within a fortnight the house had new residents.

In the small community they were part of, it didn't take long for others to register their presence. The new residents appeared to be quite anti-social. They were polite enough but discouraged any questions pertaining to their past. Through an ingenious mix of prying and speculation the neighbours had found out that Kabir was teaching in a university in the US. And as for his beautiful wife, no one knew whether she had a vocation before the couple moved to India or she was content being a homemaker. They usually changed the subject when personal questions were posed to either of them. The one thing public about them was that they seemed to like taking long walks and were often seen outdoors during the afternoon.

Samir was the first and only friend they made in the one-and-a-half years they had lived in the sleepy town. He too had a reputation of being a recluse although he was unfailingly polite to everybody. Especially to the rather large population of widows the town had. They held him in good regard although it was difficult to tell whether the respect accorded was because he was an artist or due to his affluent family background.

The town left him alone. They thought he was a bit eccentric to live alone in a cottage like that when he could easily stay in the palatial family mansion in Coimbatore and be waited on hand and foot by a retinue of servants. But then artists are meant to be a little strange. There was a woman who used to come to cook and clean for him. She had stopped working for him when Sujala moved in with Samir after she came back to Coonoor without Kabir, but that happened much later.

When Samir was first seen accompanying the couple on their walks, tongues had started to wag . Especially because it was noticed that Sujala and Samir were always talking to each other and giggling while Kabir walked a little apart from them, looking on indulgently. Malicious tongues had started hinting at a ménage à trois. The three individuals who were at the centre of this salacious speculation seemed to be hardly bothered. They seemed happy and carefree in the world they had created for themselves.

Soon neighbours noticed that Samir was visiting the cottage of his new friends in the afternoon with his easel and paints. He and Sujala remained in the cottage while Kabir took his afternoon walk, stopping by at the departmental store to have coffee on his way back. Although it could be easily surmised that Samir was painting a portrait of Sujala's, there was plenty of disapproval. It was widely believed he was painting her in the nude. The curtains were always drawn while the artist and his muse were at work and the frustrated whispers grew more vicious. No one confronted them but the frowns of disapproval were more than evident whenever any of them was spotted. But once again, all three seemed to be oblivious of the censure and were sometimes seen heading out of town in Samir's red Beetle.

Once it was clear that all the vile rumours and speculation was not going to have any kind of an impact on the trio, the scandal died down and there was quiet resignation, if not acceptance, of the relationship that the young man had built with the couple. In fact, some of those who had earlier been inclined to give credence to the theory that there was something perverse going on between the three changed their stance and pointed out that the friendship between Sujala and Samir had to be platonic for Kabir to endorse it so wholeheartedly.

An incident that had occurred a little over a year ago had once again changed their tolerant perception. Another couple had come looking for Kabir and Sujala. This woman seemed to be at least ten years older than her partner, who looked as if he was in his late twenties. They spoke with an American accent and hence it wasn't difficult to conclude that they had known Kabir and Sujala when they were living in the US. They had stopped at the departmental store and it was Harini, the girl who worked there, who had given them directions to Kabir and Sujala's cottage.

Instead of thanking her for her help, the young man had gone crazy in the store, flinging about the plastic tables and chairs and screaming at the top of his voice. Fortunately the owner, Qasim, was not present at the store, otherwise he would have definitely called in the police. The tall woman had managed to pacify him and apologized to Harini. She had also checked with the frightened girl whether they needed to pay for any damages. Harini had been far too traumatized to give any cogent response. She had asked the woman to return later and check with Qasim. Kabir had come down with her the next morning and apologized to Qasim as well as Harini for his friend's behaviour the previous day. The shrewd Qasim had claimed ten thousand rupees in damages.

Samir was in the cottage when the visitors had landed up. The neighbour, Mrs Sridhar could sense something was amiss because of the raised voices. The same night, Samir had been attacked viciously by the young man and admitted to hospital. By the time he was discharged all four of them had disappeared, locking up the cottage. Samir was shattered at this betrayal and would often drive down to their cottage and not finding his friends home check with Mrs Sridhar if she had any news about them. No one knew when they had left and certainly no one had any clue about when they would return. If at all everyone expected Samir to know where his friends had gone.

Suddenly there had been a wave of sympathy for Samir. Most residents of the town now believed that the couple were charlatans and had set up home in Coonoor only to dupe Samir. The general consensus was that Kabir and Sujala were con artists and moved from one small town to another to ensnare the heirs of large family fortunes.

As if to prove the rumour-mongers wrong Sujala had returned after a month and taken up residence in the cottage she used to occupy with her husband. When neighbours asked about Kabir, she was evasive. Samir started visiting her regularly, much to the consternation of the self-appointed moral brigade of the town. A new theory gained ground that the couple who had come visiting was related to Sujala, maybe a brother and an older sister and they had been summoned by Kabir to talk Sujala out of the relationship with Samir as it had started to threaten his marriage. There was nothing to substantiate the rumours that flew around.

Among all the speculation on the unusual closeness between the three, the last conjecture seemed to hit the mark. Sure enough, Sujala moved in with Samir. They were often seen taking walks in the afternoon. Most noticed that while Samir seemed deliriously happy, she was a pale ghost of the vivacious woman who used to talk and giggle with Samir, when Kabir had been around. They assumed that this was because the guilt of deserting her husband was weighing her down.

After a few weeks, Sujala had started working as a teacher in the school Karla ran. Folks knew about Karla's friendship with Vrinda and so it didn't take long for them to figure out who was instrumental in getting her the job. The school was an all-girls boarding and eyebrows were raised at having a woman of dubious moral character teach young, impressionable minds. But being boarders, the students were not from the town and their parents took no part in the extended gossip sessions that took place over the bridge table in the local club.

As far as Sujala and Samir were concerned, everything had seemed fine initially but over a period of time it was observed that Samir was growing increasingly moody and irritable. He may not have been friends with the residents of the town but he had been unfailingly polite to them, nodding at and wishing them whenever he bumped into anybody. Now he started rebuffing anyone who tried to make conversation. The general consensus was that Sujala was a destructive woman and had managed to spoil the young artist.

The relationship between Karla and Samir had deteriorated too. Karla lived in a small bungalow on the school campus and Sujala started visiting her on the weekends. The wagging tongues now claimed that she had begun to tire of the young besotted man and sought the older woman's company to keep away from him.

One evening Samir had barged into Karla's house and literally dragged a protesting Sujala out. She had moved back to her own cottage after that episode and when Samir dropped in uninvited she didn't let him in. Once he had banged continuously on her door for more than an hour until his hand started to bleed. He had the sympathy of the entire town. They had never approved of Sujala and believed she had destroyed the lives of two men in the span of a year.

However, one fine morning the shocked neighbours woke up to find Kabir back. The couple resumed their relationship and things went back to being the way it used to be when they had first moved in. It was clear that they no longer desired Samir's company. The first time he visited them, he was inside the cottage for not more than ten minutes; the second time, the neighbours who witnessed the incident claimed, he was not even let into the house by Kabir.

Samir lost all vestiges of dignity after Kabir's return. He spent the mornings lurking around their cottage and if they set out on a walk, he followed them at a distance. They ignored him. On the rare occasion that Sujala stepped out on her own, he tried to waylay her and strike up a conversation but she always shook him off, even when he begged and pleaded with her. His eyes were always red-rimmed from a lack of sleep and he never shaved. Vrinda and Randeep dropped in to counsel him every now and then, but he seemed to discourage their visits.

According to Mrs Kashyap, this drama continued for a couple of months before Samir saw reason. Just as suddenly as he had slipped into this self-destructive phase, he pulled himself out of it. He shaved off his beard and stopped hanging around the cottage of the woman he was so hopelessly besotted with. He stopped stalking her and the old residents of the town proudly clucked that his worthy genes had ensured that he recovered from the evil spell the promiscuous woman had cast on him. He resumed painting and often neighbours spotted him in his garden where he would set up his easel and paint in the natural light.

All was normal, until the day Karla was murdered and Samir was found at the crime scene.

There is too much of information to be processed at one go and Mrs Kashyap's propensity to ramble doesn't help. The antique clock on the wall chimes to tell me I have spent nearly two hours with her and I better leave before I overstay my welcome. I get up to go although she insists I have lunch with her. She is obviously lonely and craves company. But listening to her has disoriented me and I am not sure whether I will be able to endure her high-pitched voice for another hour. I excuse myself saying Vrinda has organized my lunch from the club and that I will take a rain check on her offer.

She walks me to the gate.

The first thing that strikes me on entering the living-room is that someone has been there in my absence. It is just an intuition. There are no visible signs of intrusion. And yet the uncomfortable feeling persists. I am drawn to the staircase that leads to the studio. It is as if an invisible force is pulling me there. The studio looks undisturbed too.

It's only when I look around again that I realize that the portrait is missing. So is the rope that lay concealed in one corner, all coiled up.

Samir has always teased me about my ability to doze off the moment I have too many things to worry about. Sleep is my antidote to anxiety. The more stressed I am, the longer I can sleep. I guess it helps to shut out the world.

I am still feeling uneasy about everything I have learnt about Samir from his neighbour. Coming back and discovering that an intruder has access to the cottage hasn't helped. Strangely, I am not afraid. I have lost my mother and everything that I have learnt after coming here tells me I am likely to lose Samir as well. I don't have anyone left to grieve over my demise, should the murderer decide to have a go at me.

I am not sure whether I should believe everything Mrs Kashyap has told me. But on the other hand, even if she exaggerated a bit, there has to be some truth to her story. Meeting Sujala in the morning also makes me believe what she has told me. She is the sort of a woman men would lose their heads over and Samir is certainly no match for her.

Knowing we are just a phone call away has made Samir and I take each other for granted. In the past year-and-a-half, since both of us were in relationships, we hardly communicated. Because my mother was murdered, I tended to believe that all the bad things happened only to me and that Samir could have been a little more sensitive to the tragedies I had encountered. Now I am learning I have been equally offhand about a major crisis in his life.

There is plenty of evidence to suggest Samir is the murderer of two single middle-aged women. He has been aggressed upon and he has also displayed bouts of aggression towards Sujala and Karla. But if someone tried to kill him yesterday in that accident, it is possible he is being framed.

Just as I start to comfort myself, I am once again assailed by another disturbing thought. Given Vrinda's influence, could this accident have been stage-managed by her? With the entire city at her disposal, she can buy the police, the doctors in the hospital, almost anyone. Maybe Samir wasn't even in the car when the accident happened. It could be an impostor who is in hospital right now. After all, I never saw him as they only allowed Vrinda inside the ICU. Maybe Samir has already absconded. Maybe he came back to take away the painting and the rope that could have implicated him.

Maybe that's the reason Vrinda wants me to leave town.

I am woken yet again by the phone. It is Vrinda calling to tell me Samir had regained consciousness for a few minutes. He had been confused and disoriented, though. 'I don't think there is any point in you coming to the hospital this evening. We will pick you up on our way back. I hope you are all packed. We are planning to shift Samir to Coimbatore tomorrow. The doctors have agreed,' she says.

'I would have liked to meet him before I left.'

'I don't think you would be able to,' she says, her tone noticeably gentler. 'The hospital rules don't allow nonfamily members inside the ICU and even if I requested them to make an exception in your case, seeing him like that will only distress you.'

'But I want to see him once before I leave,' I insist stubbornly.

'I have booked your return ticket. Your flight leaves from Coimbatore at noon,' she says as she disconnects.

I sit with the phone in my hand, my heart thudding.

Two strangers came to town

R eason is the first ally to desert you when the context is familiar but the events unpredictable. I am no stranger to the hills having spent over a dozen years in a school that was only twenty kilometres away. We were brought here by the teachers to play basketball and tennis tournaments with other boarding schools, for picnics and treks, apart from all the trips I made with Vrinda and Samir. Somehow driving up the hills from school always filled me with elation. Unlike the drive to the school from the plains after the vacations. The touch of the cold crisp air, as I sat near the window in a bus full of chatter and bonhomie, made me feel liberated from the brooding person I knew myself to be.

This trip has changed all that.

I don't know who or what to trust anymore. It is like I am lost in a dark tunnel blindly groping for support while dangers lurk all around me. I am constantly fidgeting. One part of me wants all this to end as soon as possible. Another part is afraid of what the disclosures may hold.

This long preamble is to explain my behaviour after the phone call from Vrinda. I don't think I set out of the cottage with a pre-determined agenda in my head. But there must have been some latent subconscious message that directed me to the departmental store I had visited the previous evening. The girl who had attended to me when I was there the previous day gives me a smile of recognition. The man behind the counter is absent. Maybe he is still to wake up from his afternoon siesta.

I ask the girl for a sandwich and a cup of coffee. When she brings them for me, I invite her to sit with me while I have my meal.

'Mr Qasim does not like it if I talk too much to the customers.'

'He is not here right now,' I reassure her.

'But he can come anytime and if he sees me talking to you, he will blow a fuse.' She thinks for a moment and then turns to me. 'I can stand and talk to you. In case he comes in, you can pretend that you called out to me to place an order.'

I smile at her. The smallest of actions in this town are fed by conspiracy.

'You are staying in that artist's house, aren't you?' she asks.

Taken aback by her question, it is my turn to ask her how she knows where I am staying.

'My cousin works for Mrs Kashyap. She saw you and told me a new girl was in the artist's house. When you came here yesterday and asked about him, I realized you must be the same person.'

'So all you young girls keep a tab on Samir?'

'My cousin is not young. She is married with two children.'

'And you?'

'I am not married,' she says. After a pause she adds, 'He is so good looking. He is even more handsome than a film hero. They say he comes from a very rich family in Coimbatore. We don't understand why he is living in this town. There is nothing here. And even Lakshmi has stopped working for him. So he is doing all the cooking and cleaning himself.'

I decide this is as good a time to tap her for some information. I ask her whether she knows any of the friends Samir has in the place. Her eyes turn wary. 'I can't tell you all that,' she says turning to go.

'But he is very friendly with that man who came in last night and his wife, isn't he?' I persist.

'Why do you want to know all this?' she asks turning back. 'Are you going to marry him?'

I laugh. 'Marry Samir? Certainly not. He is just a friend.'

She looks puzzled.

'What's the matter?' I ask her. 'Can't a boy and a girl be friends?'

'If my mother sees me talking to a boy, I am bound to get a beating before she goes to sleep that night,' Harini says with a smile. The banter relaxes the tension between the two of us. She is more forthcoming now. 'He was very friendly with them. Actually, Mr Dayal is a very nice man. But people say his wife is not a good woman. She has no character. When her husband was not in town she started living with the artist and when he came back, she dumped your friend. He suffered so much.'

It is on the tip of my tongue to say that maybe Samir

deserved all that suffering for getting enamoured with a married woman. But I decide against it. The girl seems half in love with Samir herself.

'Some women are like that. They possess black magic to trap men,' Harini says philosophically.

I start to laugh and then stop myself.

The black magic part of it is far-fetched but I have known women who can twirl men around their little finger. My mother had that ability. When she entered a room, all the men present had eyes only for her. She had them eating out of her hands in seconds. I used to hate going anywhere with her because of the effect she had, especially on the male of the species.

It was as if the person accompanying her did not exist for them. I know my shrink had been trying to tell me all along that my low self-esteem is because of my unresolved issues about the sensuality my mother exuded.

Lost in my thoughts, I don't realize Harini has moved away and is arranging a shelf that stocks cosmetic products. I call out to her. She comes to my table looking a bit uncertain. She knows I am trying to extract information from her.

'Do you know where they stay?'

'Who?' she says. Even though I am sure she knows who I am referring to.

'Samir's friends,' I answer nonchalantly.

She mulls the question and realizes giving directions to someone's house is not likely to land her in trouble.

'Third house on the second lane to the right when you come out of the shop. Their cottage is painted yellow. She had it re-done when they moved. You can't miss it.' She goes back to arranging the items on the shelf. Just as well, because Qasim walks in at that moment.

I stand in front of her cottage, gathering the courage to go in. I notice there are prying neighbours here too. The movement behind the curtain follows the same pattern as in Mrs Kashyap's house. I smile thinking my new friend, Samir's neighbour, is going to learn pretty soon that I had gone visiting Samir's ex. I decide there is no point in lurking outside. I might as well get it over with. I make my way to the door and for a moment all kinds of doubts assail me. What if Kabir or Sujala are rude with me for barging into their house without any notice? I tell myself what I need to find out is far greater than social niceties. Besides, Sujala had dropped in unannounced too, earlier this morning.

As I stand hesitating in the porch the front door opens. The same man who had come into the store the other night is standing before me and the scrutiny he puts me through makes me flinch. I smile tentatively at him and wait for him to invite me in. But he just stands there watching me until Sujala appears behind him. She hasn't changed after coming back. We stare at each other not knowing what to say. They stand there for some time without moving. Maybe both of them are trying to figure out whether I am a friend or an adversary.

I know I should say something to break the ice, but words fail me. Thankfully Sujala decides to end the impasse. 'It is Neha, Samir's friend. Please ask her to come in, Kabir.'

He moves reluctantly aside to let me in. I am once again conscious of the quiet strength this man possesses. Samir with all his good looks can never be a match to the security Kabir can provide a woman. He is so aristocratic, like a hero from an epic film.

'Please sit down,' Sujala says doubtfully. I can make out she is in a bit of a quandary. Since she had visited me in the morning and I went through all that trouble to return her earring, she cannot be rude and straightaway ask me the reason behind my visit. She has to engage in some small talk and I guess that is difficult for her while her husband stands there looking at both of us.

I help matters by bursting into tears. I have no idea why I am crying. Maybe it is the accumulated stress of the past few days. Kabir responds first. He goes inside and emerges with a glass of water and quietly hands it to me while his wife watches helplessly. However hard I try, I am unable to stop. She gets up from where she is sitting and comes and sits next to me.

'Hush...' she says, gathering me in her arms. It could very well be Samir who is holding me. Her touch carries the same comfort. I have no idea how long I continue to sob like that. When I come back to the world around me, I discover Kabir is sitting opposite me, looking at me indulgently. My fragility has thawed him. I am sure I am blushing and crying simultaneously. Kabir goes inside to get me a cup of steaming coffee.

'Never believe what they say about caffeine,' he jokes. 'It can be the only lifesaver in certain situations.'

'You shouldn't mind him,' Sujala says brightly. 'He doesn't mean to be insensitive. But you must tell us what is bothering you so much.'

I start to choke again.

'Easy,' Kabir says. 'You don't have to tell us if you don't want to.'

'All I want to find out is whether Samir had anything to do with my mother's murder.' There I have said it. I cannot believe I am trusting strangers with a piece of information I hold so precious. They look bewildered. Once again, it is Kabir who is the first to react. He looks at me keenly until understanding dawns in his sharp eyes.

'You mean to say...?' he says slowly.

I nod looking at him.

'What is she saying?' Sujala cries out.

Kabir continues to look at me even as he responds to his wife: 'Her mother has been murdered too. And she thinks Samir may be responsible for that death as well.'

'I know about her mother. It was a long time ago. Samir told me about it after I came back,' Sujala says walking towards me slowly and deliberately. 'Just because they are saying Samir killed Karla, you shouldn't believe that he had anything to do with your mother's murder. I know Samir was in Lucknow when that happened. But he had gone there for something else.' She draws her breath in. 'In fact he went to meet your mother to trace *me.* He thought your dad, with all the political clout he has, would be able to find out where I had gone.'

I notice that the warmth in Kabir's eyes has been replaced with the wariness that he had when he greeted me at the door.

Sujala wants to accompany me to the hospital. It has taken me some time to recover from my senseless crying. But once I have controlled myself sufficiently to know I am not going to relapse into the silly whining, fortified no doubt by the strong coffee and the numerous tissues Sujala has pressed into my hands, I am in touch with something I find hard to put in words. I have started feeling comfortable in Samir's ex girlfriend's house and that awareness is confusing to say the least. I should be hostile towards this woman for causing all the upheavals in Samir's life. Instead I feel like taking care of her myself.

I have never had a problem adjusting to any new space but the absolute sense of ease I have with this couple, who are relative strangers, is something new. It's not as if they have gone to any trouble to make me feel at home. On the contrary, they talk to each other as if I am not in the same room. Sujala is sitting on Kabir's lap, occasionally nuzzling his neck while she pauses for my response.

I talk to her about Vrinda. About how fond I have been of her and how unreasonable she has turned out to be of late. I add I have no idea how Vrinda would react to me going to the hospital when she had asked me not to. What I omit to say is that if Sujala accompanies me and Vrinda runs into us, she is likely to call hospital security and have us thrown out.

Now that I have been relieved of all the tension I have been carrying within me, thanks to all that confiding and crying, I have turned more alert to my surroundings and check out the living room where we are all sitting.

It is clear the mistress of the house is partial to yellow. The upholstery on the sofa and the cushions are a pale lemon. The curtains are blue sprinkled with tiny yellow paisley. One corner of the room has an oval-shaped wooden table with four chairs. The tablemats are in grey and yellow.

A large intricately-carved wooden Ganesha stands in one corner and one wall has shelves filled with blue pottery and marble and ivory figurines.

'We got this place with the furniture. Her children only took away the crystal,' the smile is back on Kabir's face as he follows my eyes.

I smile back at him and tell them I should leave.

'I am coming with you,' Sujala interjects, getting up from Kabir's lap. I nod tiredly at her.

I tell myself it has been a while since I bothered about the consequences of my actions. Why start now?

The hospital has many visitors at this time of the day. They are all trooping in to visit their relatives – young mothers with new-born babies; the old making a last-ditch effort to survive. I am sure the two of us look incongruous. We are too dissimilar to pass as relatives – there is no way anyone can confuse the two of us to be a part of the same condoling family – but I experience a curious kinship with Sujala. I am unable to explain it. I am still finding it difficult to shake off the light-headedness I have been feeling since I have been at their house.

We approach the nurse's station outside the ICU. An irritable looking nurse looks at us suspiciously. 'How is Samir Moodoor doing now?' Sujala enquires.

'Are you family?' the nurse wearing a badge that says Janet asks sternly.

'No. We are friends of the family.'

'I am sorry. We have strict instructions from the police not to disclose any information of accident patients to anyone except members of the immediate family. Especially in this case.'

'What is so special about this case?' it is my turn to ask.

She opens her mouth and shuts it again. A ward boy comes out of the ICU. Both Sujala and I turn at the same time and try to catch a glimpse of the patients inside. The two beds we can spot from the outside are facing the other way. The man notices us staring and closes the door hurriedly. The nurse is frowning at him.

'All I want to know is Samir's condition. How is he?' I plead with her.

'Where have you been? I have been calling you since the last two hours. Can't you at least respond?' says Vrinda from behind me. Even as I turn in confusion I can hear the annoyance in her voice. Vrinda starts to smile at me and then checks herself as soon as she realizes Sujala has accompanied me.

'I thought I made it clear that hospital rules do not allow for any visitors apart from the immediate family,' she adds coldly.

Neither of us can argue with that.

Sujala turns to me, 'I may as well go. Please keep me posted about Samir's condition. Take care,' she calls out and leaves without looking at Vrinda.

'You have still not told me why you didn't respond to my calls,' Vrinda turns on me angrily.

I want to tell her I am grown up now. I am no longer the young schoolgirl who used to visit with her son. Instead I dig into my bag and take out my mobile phone. The battery has died. I have forgotten to charge my phone since yesterday. I wave the phone under her nose. 'That's why,' I say triumphantly.

'I am going inside to check on Samir,' Vrinda coldly responds.

'Can I come with you?' I ask.

She stops when she hears my request and shakes her head in exasperation. 'Please wait here,' she says and goes inside the room shutting the door firmly behind her.

I look at the nurse who is busy scribbling something. There is a half smile playing on her lips. She seems pleased at the snub Vrinda has given me.

After some time, Vrinda emerges from the ICU; her face is inscrutable.

'He's the same, not much improvement since morning,' she says when I check with her about Samir's condition. We drive back to the cottage to collect my bag. On the way I try to tell her there is no point in me shifting to the club for just one evening but she ignores my protests.

The man at the reception cannot stop fawning over Vrinda as I sign the register and take the key. An attendant emerges from the corridors and insists on taking my bag to my room on the first floor. Vrinda tells me we will meet in the dining room in half an hour. The phone rings in her bag just then. She fishes it out and frowns when she sees who is calling. She moves to a side to take her call while I follow the man who is carrying my bag.

The room is large with a high ceiling. For the first time since I have come here I feel I have a right to the space I am in. It exists to offer hospitality to strangers. The smells contained in it are anonymous. I may be staying here as a guest of Vrinda's but there is security in the thought that she does not own the club. The thought fortifies me. I feel I can take charge of my life again. I will not allow Vrinda to dictate the course of the dinner we are going to have together. She wants to run the life of everyone around her. I can understand why Sujala dislikes her. I am sure all of Samir's girlfriends have had to battle Vrinda's disapproval. I have been lucky only because she has never thought of me as someone who could have a romantic relationship with her precious son.

That thought is enough to have me raging again. I will make sure she sees a different side of me when we meet for dinner.

Dine in haste...

I enter the dining room only to find Vrinda is not there. Instead, Randeep is seated alone at a table.

A young couple and two small children are the only other guests present. They look up as I come in and the woman smiles at me. I force a smile as I make my way to Randeep. He gets up and waits until I am seated. He has always been unfailingly polite as far as I can remember. Even on his wedding day, he had bent to pick up the scarf that had slipped from my shoulders. Samir calls his stepfather a fake but I have always appreciated this aspect of him. He is one of the few men who did not take too much time to figure out I am a woman.

He apologizes profusely for Vrinda not being there. 'She is on a conference call with an overseas client,' he says. 'It may take time so she sent me ahead.' A man wearing a bow tie and a butler's coat comes and stands next to our table with a little pad and pen in his hand. Randeep orders for the two of us after checking with me: 'They don't do anything fancy here, but the chef is reliable. If you don't mind, can I order since I happen to know his success rate with different dishes?'

I nod at him disinterestedly. I have never been too much of a food person. It is Samir who fancies himself a gourmet cook. I am always glad to leave the ordering to someone else when I am eating out. Especially in capable hands such as Randeep's, as he pauses only to ask me whether I would prefer red or white wine and chicken or lamb as the main course.

Once the man leaves with the order, Randeep smiles at me. It occurs to me this is the first time we have been alone like this. I can count the times I have met him earlier on my fingers and Vrinda has always been present. I wonder what we can find in common to talk about until his wife joins us.

To make matters worse, the information Samir has shared with me about his stepfather's brutal side comes to haunt me at that moment. I can picture him sitting in his car and rolling up the window with the urchin's hand in it. I shudder involuntarily and hope he hasn't noticed my discomfort.

Fortunately for me he misunderstands my gesture. 'Are you cold?' he asks. 'All this must be very stressful for you.' I smile and look away. Maybe the story Samir told me about his stepfather is not true. After all, he has told me so many untruths over the years.

Luckily for me, Randeep does not appear to be a very perceptive man. He continues to talk, telling me about how he was in Bombay on some work when Vrinda called to tell him that Samir had been arrested. He says he got onto the next flight. 'I don't think Samir cares for me too much, but I do think of him as the son I never had,' he admits ruefully. He looks so vulnerable at that moment that I feel like reassuring him. I have this thing for older men; I am sure Freud would have something to say about this.

Randeep seems to be in the mood to ramble and he goes on and on about all the attempts he has made to reach out to Samir. 'He was seventeen when Vrinda and I were married. I am aware that is a tough age for someone to have to get used to the fact that his mother is going to have a new man in her life.'

I am finding it difficult to stem the flood of nostalgia from my companion that involves his various attempts to win favour with an unrelenting stepson. Thankfully the food arrives just then.

The food and wine vouch for his good taste, though. The red wine he has ordered is smooth and comforts me as it slides down my throat. When I compliment him about it, he says it is Argentinean.

'Terrazas Reserva Malbec,' he announces with pride. 'I love the smooth finish it has. They stock it here only because they know Vrinda and I are partial to it.' The chicken liver paté with olives is a perfect starter. For the main course he has ordered grilled lamb chops for me and lamb stroganoff for himself.

'The chef makes an exception in my case. Usually they do the beef stroganoff, but I have never touched beef in my life. My only concession to religion,' he laughs. I don't know whether it is the wine or the exotic lamb chops, but soon I am talking as much as Randeep. Sharing with him all the confusions I am living, with regard to Samir. I have

always prided myself on being a private person. The reason
I don't have any close friends apart from Samir owes to the
fact that I find it impossible to open up about my innermost
feelings and thoughts. All my boyfriends in the past have
always complained that they never really knew where they
stood with me. Not that there have been very many. The
count is three to date, including that slime-ball, Subbu. But
this is the second time in one day that I am opening up
like this to a stranger.

His phone rings just then and he frowns. He apologizes
saying, 'I never take calls when I have company for dinner,
but Vrinda asked me to make an exception tonight as she
wanted to keep me posted about when she will be joining
us.'

He listens silently for some time and grunts an okay
before hanging up. 'That was Vrinda,' he admits, the note
of apology back in his voice. 'She says her tele-conference
was disrupted by network problems and is going to resume
in a few minutes. She won't be able to join us.'

I am so angry that I almost choke. I am sure she is
snubbing me on purpose to punish me for coming to the
hospital with Sujala. I tell myself I am not going to let her
off so easily. I shall give Randeep a hard time instead of her
and hope that he reports whatever we have discussed to a
disbelieving Vrinda. By the time the desserts arrive – a fig
and pistachio tart for me and a chocolate mousse cake for
Randeep – I have found the courage to ask him whether
he thinks Samir is guilty.

He averts his face when he hears the question. When he
turns to me again, his eyes are full of anguish. 'How do you
expect me to answer that question? I love that boy. I was

87

married earlier. I am sure you know that. I had a son who died when he was seven. He fell off the roof of my ancestral home. It broke up my first marriage and caused my wife and me to separate. We couldn't bear to go on living under the same roof, each holding the other responsible.' He takes a moment to compose himself. 'You have no idea what the loss of a child does to the parents.'

'I do know what the murder of a parent does to the child,' the words are out of my mouth before I can stop them.

An awkward silence settles between us. Neither of us is interested in talking any more. Both of us are pretending to concentrate on the food. I am sure Randeep is cursing himself for getting himself into this situation. I, on the other hand, have the satisfaction of knowing that Vrinda is going to squirm in discomfort when Randeep reports our conversation to her.

She will know I still suspect her son. For some reason that thought gives me immense pleasure. It is as if I have transferred all the hostility I used to feel towards my mother to Vrinda and the warmth I used to carry towards my friend's mother now engulfs my dead mother. I am trying to redeem a relationship in retrospect, long after the person has left this world.

Suddenly Randeep leans across to me. 'It may surprise you how little I know about the woman I have been married to for the last eight years – forget her son. It is as if I am the perennial outsider. You have no idea how similar Vrinda and Samir are in most respects. There is a part of them that is all head – no heart.'

The way he describes them sends a shiver down my body. In a way, he has articulated my unspoken thoughts. My heart is thudding once again. I am impatient to hear a few more confessions from him that will help settle my doubts once and for all. But he turns silent after that, beckoning to the waiter to get the cheque that he signs distractedly.

Afterwards he insists on walking me to my room. It is obvious that he never lets his courtesy desert him, regardless of the provocation. He turns to go once I let myself into my room with a good night. As I am beginning to latch the door from inside, there is a gentle tap. He is standing there looking distraught. I draw my breath in, nervous, not quite knowing what is causing the anxiety within me.

'You asked me something,' he begins. 'I have been battling with the same question ever since Samir was arrested.'

'Why don't you come in,' I say noticing that the family who was dining with us has come up just then. The man is opening a door that is two rooms removed from mine, while the woman is staring at us with a strange look on her face. The kids are lost in their own world, whispering something to each other and giggling. Maybe she has me down as the older man's mistress. I glare at her until she looks away.

Randeep is oblivious to our silent exchange. Whatever he has to say is taking a lot out of him. He comes into the room closing the door gently behind him. 'I feel terrible about saying this but maybe you should go back tomorrow as Vrinda wants you to. Go and meet your father. I am sure he is doing something to avenge your mother's murder. After all, they were together for many years.'

I give a derisive snort and look away. 'Knowing my father, he must have replaced her with a younger mistress by now.'

'Now you are being unfair. I have no idea why everyone in your generation thinks of our generation as being a thoroughly insensitive lot,' he says impatiently and leaves the room without wishing me goodnight.

The man has forgotten his manners for once.

I have been kidding myself that I haven't been able to sleep for the last few days because of my complex feelings towards Samir. I was wrong, of course. Now that I cannot see or talk to him, I have realized what I have been dealing with all along is the intensity of memory. I have been living in the past, all the years we spent together in school. We have met a few times in Delhi in the past two years when he would come down for shows and exhibitions but we had taken each other for granted, like any pair of childhood friends.

This trip is different because nostalgia lit it like a flickering candle. I turned seventeen again and saw Samir crying like a baby in my presence because his mother was getting married, but of course that was a different Samir. He was vulnerable at that time and not a suspect in the murder of my mother. I would rather have had our relationship frozen in time, so I could continue to love him. But this elusive stranger who may or may not be in the hospital recuperating right now, is not someone I want to meet again. Sleeping on this alien bed away from his house has freed me. I may have cured myself after all.

This time she is present in the dining room, having breakfast with Randeep. I find it difficult to shake off the dislike I am developing towards her. Samir had once called his mother a control freak. I had protested then but now I can understand what he meant. If Samir has been going around murdering women his mother's age, I don't think I need to qualify as a shrink to understand why he is doing so. I might even have felt a twinge of sympathy for him if he had spared my mother.

Randeep, after a forced greeting, averts his face. He is looking visibly uncomfortable. I guess after what he encouraged me to do last night, guilt has set in. After all he came close to implicating his beloved wife's son in not one, but two murders. I wonder what it must be like for him; being caught in the crossfire between an over-possessive mother and a rebellious son.

The national press is yet to get wind of Karla's murder and the fact that Samir is the prime suspect. The town being what it is and Vrinda's overwhelming influence, the news of the murder itself must have been played down so much that no one outside the town would even know a woman has been murdered.

My chain of disparate thoughts is broken by the waiter asking me how I would like to have my eggs.

'Fried,' says Vrinda. 'She likes them sunny side up.'

'An omelette please,' I interrupt. I don't like omelettes and Vrinda no doubt remembers that from the countless breakfasts she supervised for Samir and me when we were children. I have embarked on a private little revolution. To let her know at every stage that she is wrong about me.

I have underestimated her. As soon as we are done with breakfast Vrinda informs me that Samir has been flown to a hospital in Coimbatore early in the morning in a private aircraft. She would have accompanied him, but with Samir being on a stretcher and a doctor and nurse accompanying him, there was no place for her.

'The good thing is they have landed and he is already in the new hospital with better facilities. He has not yet recovered but the doctors in Coimbatore are optimistic...' she trails off.

If I had any lingering doubt about Samir's complicity in the two murders, it disappears at that moment. I know he is guilty and she is covering for him. Accusing her at that moment is out of the question. I find my eyes welling up. She has disarmed me completely. There is no way I can accuse her of what I believe in my heart. She is the worried, anxious mother at this moment and if I confront her with my unsubstantiated allegations, I am the one who is going to be seen as unreasonable; it is not as if she is going to meekly agree to whatever I say.

Choked with emotion, I look at Randeep for support. He is concentrating on his breakfast and pretending he has not heard a word.

Vrinda turns businesslike. 'A car has been arranged to drop you to the Coimbatore airport. It will probably take around one-and-a-half to two hours to reach. You should check out of here in another half an hour. Your flight departs fifteen minutes past noon and it is almost nine now. We are leaving too, but I have to go to the police station first and inform them about moving Samir. I have been told the station in-charge will be coming in only by ten thirty.'

What can I say to her? In any case, what is the point of staying on if Samir isn't in town anymore? That is, if he was ever admitted to the hospital. More likely, Vrinda has secreted him away in a safe hiding place.

The best course of action available to me for now is to follow instructions.

She never really died

I returned to Delhi a fortnight ago and I have dreamt of
her every night. It is a strange kind of a dream. Parts of
it are happy even though it ends in a nightmare:

*Sujala and I are in Samir's garden bending over the Kurinji
bushes. We are marvelling at the colour and the way Samir has
domesticated the shrub. Both of us notice the fallen earring at the
same time. We bend to pick it together and our heads collide. We
start laughing and walk inside the cottage holding hands. She leaves
me sitting on the sofa and goes inside Samir's room. I wait for her
impatiently. I want to tell her something and wish she would hurry.
I notice the door of Samir's room opening. It is not her but Samir
who emerges from the room, his eyes bloodshot. He is dragging her
body by the neck of her dress. She leaves a trail of blood and when
Samir dumps the body triumphantly in front of me, I notice that
her hands are tied in a gesture of supplication...*

I always wake up sweating at this point and spend the
rest of the night pacing the house.

I have called up Vrinda twice after coming back to check
whether Samir has recovered. She has taken my call both
times to tell me that he is still in a coma but the doctors

are optimistic about his recovery. I never fail to get angry after talking to her. If he is still unconscious, how come she manages to sound so calm and detached? I remember how worried she had looked the day I reached Coonoor. And how matter-of-fact she had been on the day I was leaving. If at all, things had gone from bad to worse for Samir in the days that followed, so how could she have turned calmer? She must think I am an absolute idiot to believe her son is in hospital.

It is a Sunday morning and I wake up to the persistent ringing of the doorbell. I had fallen asleep with great difficulty after coming back sloshed the previous evening from an office party; images from the days I'd recently spent in Coonoor kept playing in my head. I sit up on my bed, my head throbbing with pain. I throw a robe over my flimsy night-dress and stumble out of bed.

There is a young man at the door. He is dressed in formal clothes. A white and blue pin-striped shirt with navy blue trousers and black leather shoes. I shut the door on his face and make my way to the intercom to scream at the security at the gate. They have strict instructions not to let salesmen into the building without checking with the residents. But the ringing of the doorbell resumes, more persistent than ever, driving me nuts. I go back to the door and open it. The idiot is grinning from ear to ear.

'I am not interested,' I scream at him. 'Whatever you may be selling.'

'Sorry, Madam,' he responds brightly. 'I am not a salesman. I am Veer Chaturvedi. IPS. Sub-divisional police officer from Lucknow. I am investigating the murder of your mother,' and he flashes his ID.

I stand there and gawk at him not comprehending why he has landed up on my doorstep in Delhi on a Sunday morning.

I have no option but to invite him in. I excuse myself on the pretext of making some coffee for both of us. I put the kettle to boil and hurriedly go into my room and change into a shirt and a pair of jeans. I go back to the kitchen and emerge with two steaming mugs of coffee.

'I don't drink tea or coffee,' he says when I offer him a mug. 'Only milk.'

I am not quite sure what I am supposed to do when he says that. Is he expecting me to fetch him a glass of milk? As if guessing my thoughts he hastens to add, 'No, no, please do not bother. I have only two glasses a day. Once in the morning and once before I go to bed.'

I have no idea how to deal with this clown of a policeman. He speaks English with a peculiar accent pointing to his small town upbringing. But he is remarkably sharp when he asks me questions. Interested and probing, unlike all the cops I had met immediately after Mother's death. He tells me my mother's murder is one in a series of crimes the state intelligence has been deputed to investigate. 'There could be a greater conspiracy than we initially suspected.'

I tell him what he is saying sounds impressive to me but unless he has something concrete to share with me about who murdered her, it is of little interest.

'You shouldn't lose faith,' he tells me grandly getting me all annoyed. 'Faith can move mountains.'

'You can keep your faith,' I retort. 'As long as I know who killed my mother.'

'So you want to get down to business?' he asks looking at me thoughtfully.

'Yes, please.'

'Very well, then. You answer the questions I am going to ask you and leave it to me to find out who killed your mother,' he concludes in a matter-of-fact tone. At least he has stopped grinning and that's an improvement.

He spends the next hour grilling me about my mother's life. What did I know about her work? Did she ever talk to me about those who were close to her? How often did we meet? Who were the people who dropped in to meet her when I was in Lucknow? Did she have any relatives I was in touch with? Family? Friends? Acquaintances? His questions seem never-ending and my aching head is of no help. I start snapping at him and am almost on the verge of asking him to leave my house when he stops and tells me that should be enough for the time being.

He gets up to leave and I trail behind him. He turns at the door suddenly. 'You don't seem to be taking good care of your health. You shouldn't neglect yourself like this. And I will do my best to get the person who did this to your mother.'

Is this guy for real?

It must be the stress I have been carrying all these days that made me behave the way I did with Pulkith today, while I was being appraised on my performance at work. Pulkith has been my boss for nearly three years now, ever since I passed out of the management institute and joined this organization. He is a decent enough man. Manages his boundaries well and is always correct in his responses. He is one of those robots organizations feel lucky to own. He plays by the rules and works as long as it is needed to get something done. He believes in norms, systems and structures and expects those who work with him to do the same.

Once a year the organization expects him to sit with the members of his team and talk to them about how they have fared during the previous twelve months and he goes through a lot of preparation beforehand to ensure the process is as smooth as can be. He comes prepared for the meetings with his notes that have clearly marked out what he has noticed about his subordinates in the past year. I am not clear whether he makes the notes as and when he observes something or he stores them in his head and jots them all down just before the meeting starts. His style is to kick off the meeting with a flaw and have a long discussion about managing what he calls the non-strengths. After which he moves on to the successes and achievements and is generally quite effusive in his praise.

I know how it works with him and so there is no surprise in the way he starts. 'Neha, before we get into the successes and achievements of the past year, there is a concern area I would like to address.'

'Please go ahead,' I urge. I am surprised at the disdain my voice holds at that moment. Even the normally thick-skinned Pulkith looks a bit surprised at my tone.

'I have observed in the past one year that your performance tends to suffer when you are undergoing personal stress.' He stops for a second when I avert my face. His tone is noticeably gentler as he continues. 'I do understand you have had to encounter a terrible tragedy. Your mother passing away suddenly like that, in an accident.'

'It wasn't an accident.'

'Sorry, I don't understand?' he says looking slightly flustered. The discussion is not going the way he anticipated.

'She was murdered. The person who killed her battered in her face and then tied her hands in front of her so she looked like she was pleading for mercy.'

He has no idea how to react to what I am saying. Different expressions flit across his face in a matter of seconds – surprise, disbelief, concern and finally something that is akin to pity. It is the one I find most unbearable. I continue relentlessly:

'I agree I should have put it all behind me as soon as it happened and got back to work doubly charged. I am sure that is what you would expect of a professional. But I am sorry that I have occasionally grieved over her and felt that she didn't deserve a death bereft of any dignity. I apologize all the more for sometimes having thought of all this even when I have been at work. That was totally unbecoming of me. How could I forget I am being paid for the time I spend here and cannot engage in personal luxuries of any kind including grief?'

'Neha, I am sorry. I didn't know,' he says looking helplessly at me.

'And what would you have come up with as your opening statement assuming you *had* known? Don't tell me you would have broken your system of starting with what you call one of my "non-strengths". I doubt it. You would have just found a nicer way of saying what you said earlier,' I cannot believe the venom with which I am spitting out my words.

'Listen, have you thought of taking professional help? If you want I can find someone,' he offers lamely.

I have had enough.

'Please don't worry. I plan to send you my resignation letter as soon as I get back to my work station,' I am sounding very tired, even to myself.

'I won't entertain it,' Pulkith splutters looking shattered.

I get up quietly and work towards the door of his cabin. On an impulse I turn back. 'You mustn't blame yourself for any of this. The meeting had nothing to do with it. I am surprised I lasted this long after all that has happened to me in the past year-and-a-half. I have other more pressing matters to attend to and your organization will not want to pay me for doing what I have to do now.'

'You don't have to resign. After what has happened to you, I will do my best to get the company to sanction you long leave,' he offers.

I consider his proposal for a split second and then shake my head.

'No. Thanks for your offer, though. I don't know how long it is going to take before I sort out my personal mess and cannot commit a definite date when I will be back. Besides, my mother left me a fortune. It's time I put it to good use. I can't think of a better way of doing it than tracking her killer.'

He knows when he is defeated. He gets up from his chair and walks towards me, extending his hand in a gesture of goodwill. Both of us force a smile. I tell Pulkith I will give a fortnight's notice and tie up whatever is pending from my side. Fortunately, I am yet to get fully into the new project I have been assigned after coming back. I can think of at least two persons whom I can hand it over to.

Sometimes we postpone the inevitable waiting for that elusive sign that tells us it's time to move on. I have to thank the young cop who dropped in unannounced last Sunday and my boss for letting me see clearly what I have been trying to ignore all along.

The hills are calling.

I come back after my last day at work to the usual.

An empty flat cleaned in my absence by the maid who lets herself in with the key she takes from the neighbour. My dinner is waiting for me in a casserole on the dining table waiting to be heated in the microwave. It feels strange somehow to be in this rented flat now that I don't have the job. The only reason I called it home was because I worked in this city and needed a place to come back to after the day's work was done. Subbu never shared this flat with me. He was gone four months when I moved in here. I know I have to give up the place now. I have never liked Delhi. It can never be home. But then the concept of home is itself alien to me.

I open the window of the living room and watch an old man and a little girl, possibly his granddaughter, walking together, her hand in his. My eyes well with tears. I have never had an extended family. If my mother had any family before she chose to be with the man, they had disowned her before I was born.

As for the man, I am sure that apart from his wife and three children, not to forget the majestic dog, he has a large brood of siblings and cousins with whom he gets together for festivals and weddings and anniversaries – occasions on which my mother and I were never welcome. He never asked us to accompany him and we never went.

Before I go to sleep I decide that I must contact him before I leave for Coonoor. The young cop talking about a conspiracy theory has left me wondering whether there was a political angle to the murder of my mother with the man involved in it somehow. Maybe he is the one who is trying to implicate Samir. I know he has a lot of enemies in his own party. My mother had mentioned it to me more than once. Have some of them got the state intelligence agencies to probe his role in the crime? So many of the questions the cop asked me seemed to deal with her relationship with the man and how closely they were associated personally and professionally.

I had caught them fighting once when I was a young girl. I had woken up in the middle of the night feeling afraid and gone looking for my mother. She was in the living room and the man was with her. He was shaking her roughly and snarling, 'I am going to kill you one of these days!' I had stood there trembling, I don't know for how long, until Mother noticed me. She had pushed him away and walked towards me, gathering me in her arms and taking me to my room and firmly latching the door behind her. I had snuggled up to her too afraid to ask anything.

The infuriating thing is that that is all I remember. Memory can be such an unreliable ally, failing you just when you have to draw on it the most. Despite all the rage I feel towards Samir I guess I have to thank him for one thing; because he's in the picture, it's not a foregone conclusion in my head that one of my parents was responsible for the death of the other. After all, what possible connection could the man have with Karla who was running a school in a far-away hill-station?

I have always had his number even though I don't remember having called him even once in my entire life. My mother had insisted I keep it when she was alive.

'I know you dislike him but he is the only one you have apart from me and you should never feel shy of approaching him. He is a good man that way. He will never refuse you.'

It takes me nearly an hour to gather my courage and call him up. The first time he doesn't pick up my call. Maybe Mother wasn't as responsible about leaving my number with him. That would be typical of her – to boast of his magnanimity to her daughter but to be afraid to mention me in his presence. She had dedicated most of her adult life to being with him. He must have taught her the political ropes she used in her personal relationships. I send him a message saying I have been trying to call him and I will be grateful if he can spare me a few minutes.

He calls back immediately. 'Ratna had given me your number but I lost my last phone and many of the numbers that were stored in it,' he says. He hesitates a little before adding, 'I am glad you called. Do you need anything?'

This is all we have left between us, I think bitterly, now that Mother is gone. A relationship defined entirely by the transaction of what I need and what he can offer. 'I wanted to know if you have been able to find out anything about who murdered Ma,' I am surprised at how matter-of-fact I manage to sound.

There is silence for a few seconds, leaving me wondering whether we have been disconnected due to network problems. But he responds eventually, sounding thoughtful, 'At first I thought her death had been engineered by my rivals to discredit me by linking me with her murder, but all the enquiries by the police in that direction proved to be futile. I am sure I too would have been a suspect but I was addressing a rally around the time of her death and afterwards had a meeting with the party workers of my constituency. So they spared me. Nor could they find anyone suspicious who could be linked directly or indirectly to me,' he adds with a wry laugh.

I wonder why he is sounding so defensive. Maybe he has guessed I have suspected him in the past.

'Truth is, they haven't been able to make much headway.'

'I am sure they will find the murderer if you pressure them. But I suppose you are more worried about the political repercussions of such a move.'

'I cared for your mother. We were together for many years,' he says and pauses. 'I have some influence with the chief minister and have got him to use the state intelligence machinery to once again probe her murder. I am doing my best,' he says before abruptly hanging up. I am not sure whether I want to believe him.

All I know is I need to make a trip to her house before I go back to Coonoor.

Making peace

Since we need words to remember it follows that our earliest memory is of a time when we have learnt to speak. Whenever I try to reminisce about my early life I seem to start much later. My memories are all about the years I spent in school and the times I would come home during the holidays, hating the man because he could be with Mother when I was miles away. She, on the other hand, has stored a past in her cupboard that dates back to a time when I didn't have the powers to register, let alone, remember anything.

There is a tiny pouch containing what I presume is my first milk tooth. A tiny thin gold chain the size of my fist and a tinier locket, a tattered book of alphabets, a pink satin frock I recognize from the pictures of my first birthday and my first pair of shoes – these are the other treasures she has stored in an embroidered cloth bag. I touch them one by one and suddenly I can smell her in the room. It is unbearable and I run out and almost collide with Jamuna who is sweeping the living room. She looks up at me, puzzled, and something akin to compassion dawns in her tired eyes.

'*Ma ki yaad aa gayi,*' she says nodding her head. I shake mine to deny what is obvious to her and go to my room and shut the door firmly behind me.

Jamuna was with Mother for nearly twenty years. She lived with her, cooked and cleaned for her. Once a year she went on three weeks' leave to her village, making sure her trip did not clash with my school holidays. In her absence, she would make sure to find a temporary replacement to do her work. The replacements were usually part-time domestic helps, who worked for the neighbours and who were happy for the extra income that working in Mother's house for three weeks provided.

The murderer had struck wisely.

He had picked his time to correspond with Jamuna's absence; all the more reason for me to believe that the murderer was someone who knew Mother, and her household routine.

I am back in the small bungalow she lived in for the last few years in one of the recently constructed hubs for the nouveau riche. The poster-boy of corruption and political wheeling-dealing has built a large palace for his beautiful middle-aged mistress in this locality. When she was younger, the mistress used to dance on top of brass vessels in South Indian films. Now they say she only dances for her paramour when she is not visiting her constituency in rural UP, her sari demurely covering her head. Mother had laughed when she'd narrated the story to me on one of my previous visits to Lucknow.

'And what do they say about *you*?' I had asked with deliberate cruelty. 'I am sure there are stories about the two of you doing the rounds too.'

She had looked away, shaming me with the distress her eyes carried. But I had hated her those days for having sold the old house in Haiderganj that was located a stone's throw from Naval Kishore Marg, which housed the school I had yearned to attend.

Most days when I was home for the holidays, I would look out of my window and wish that instead of sending me back to the hostel, Mother would keep me with her, enrolling me in a school that I could walk to every day, like I saw other young boys and girls do. They all seemed to be happier than I was.

I finally let go of that longing in high school – when I couldn't bear to be in the same room as her even during the short spells for which we were together. My anger usually peaked on the days the man came over and stayed the night. But I missed the view of the school nonetheless; it was a reminder of what my childhood could have been. The view of the Gomti could never compensate adequately for that.

I had taken Jamuna for granted in the aftermath of the murder. In any case, I didn't have her home address. But then a fortnight after Mother died, she had tracked me down to my flat in Delhi. I was on the verge of leaving for Boston on the assignment Pulkith had so thoughtfully arranged for me. Although she refused to tell me how she found out where I lived, I knew the man had something to do with it. She had sat on the floor of my house and howled miserably as I had looked on in confusion, feeling a little envious at how easily she could embrace her grief. She had stayed the night at my place and in the morning I had given her the keys to Mother's house and told her to take care of it until I decided what to do with it. I assured her I would arrange for her monthly salary to be deposited in the savings account Mother had opened for her.

I had not gone back to Lucknow in a year although she would call from time to time enquiring when I was visiting next. Sometimes I called to check whether she was fine.

Ever since I have got here, Jamuna has been forcing food down my throat, evoking memories of how Mother would always mention my favourite dishes when she sat down to eat. I am sure all the free time Jamuna has had in the last year has been well spent in front of the idiot box. The picture she paints of Mother as a sentimental soul always yearning for her daughter could well belong to the family melodramas patented by the daily soap brigade. But there seems to have been some truth to her assertion. At least that's what a cursory search of Mother's cupboard has revealed.

How often we say parents don't understand their children. The discovery of all those souvenirs from my infancy is a reminder that the converse is equally true.

My mother was a stranger to me when she lived and continues to be one in her death; we never really knew each other.

Jamuna and I settle down for a chat after dinner on the second day. I want to know from her whether Samir visited Mother often. 'Only when you were here and he came to stay for a few days. That was more than two years ago, wasn't it?' she says furrowing her brow.

'No, more recently. Didn't he visit Mother when I wasn't around?' I ask impatiently.

'I am not sure. I think she did mention he was coming to Lucknow just before I was going away,' she says, blinking back her tears. That is the trouble when I try to talk to Jamuna. She starts crying whenever Mother is mentioned. All that snivelling just gets to me after a while. For a moment I toy with the idea of telling her Samir is a suspect in Mother's murder. But no, the shock will be too much for her and God alone knows who she would repeat the information to. I am not even sure whether I want the man to know about Samir as yet.

Over the past two days, I have been through all Mother's drawers, rifling through her papers. There has to be something that would give me a clue. Something I can take back and confront Vrinda and Samir with. But I have found nothing that can link Samir to her murder.

'Are you going to live here now?' Jamuna asks me hopefully. 'Haven't you given up that job in Delhi?'

I smile at her. 'No, I don't think I can ever live in Lucknow but yes, I have given up that job in Delhi.'

She looks deflated. 'What have you decided about the house?' she asks me.

'What do you mean?'

'Are you going to sell it? Is that why you are here?' she asks tonelessly.

'I haven't thought of it.'

'In case you decide to, would you let me know beforehand? I will have to look for another job. I can go back to the village to my brother's house,' she says slowly, deliberating over each word. 'But I don't think they would be very happy if I stayed there permanently. Even now they are happy to see me because of the things I carry with me when I go to visit them. If a woman has no husband and no income, no one wants her.'

I have always blamed Mother for the compromises she made in agreeing to be the mistress of a wealthy man. Listening to Jamuna makes me understand for the first time why she did what she did. And then I tell myself Jamuna's context is very different. Mother was educated with a Masters in Economics from Allahabad University. She had a respectable job. She couldn't have been forced to take on a paramour and have his bastard. It was a choice she had exercised.

I am aware Jamuna is looking at me hopefully.

'I have no plans to sell this house in the near future, much as I hate it,' I tell her slowly. 'And so long as it is here I want you to stay and take care of it.'

She looks away broodingly. I realize I have not given her the response she is looking for.

'I have things to do right now but as and when I settle everything and decide on a home for myself, I will call you. You can always come and stay with me.'

She brightens instantly. The long familiarity we have shared prevents her from thanking me. But it is there in the way she looks at me. I spy the same fondness on her face that I noticed she had for my mother whenever I was home. It had always made me edgy back then and I often took out the anger I felt for Mother on her. This visit without Mother's physical presence in the house has been different. I have replaced Mother in her loyalty. Thinking about the hostility I bore towards Mother whenever I was home in the past few years makes me uncomfortable and I get up to wash my hands.

'His parents came, though, once for dinner,' she says, starting to collect the dishes. She always eats in the kitchen after I have finished. It was the same when Mother was alive. Despite the closeness they shared, eating at the same table was not acceptable to either of them. I wouldn't mind if Jamuna and I sat and ate together. But I am sure if I suggested it, she would be appalled.

What she says does not register until I have finished washing my hands. She is in the kitchen when I turn. I go and stand near the door as she puts my plate in the sink.

'Who came for dinner?' I ask, my heart thudding.

'Samir Bhai's parents. I was seeing them for the first time. She told me after they left that they were his parents and had come down from somewhere near Madras. It must have been six months prior to...' she gets all choked up again and I begin to get impatient with her.

'Do you have any idea why they visited Mother?' I demand.

She shakes her head. 'They were visiting Lucknow and came over. He was also present for the dinner.' Jamuna is like me in that respect. She has also not chosen any term of endearment for the man. She refers to him as 'he' just as I call him the 'man'. She gives in to a bout of nostalgia again.

'I cooked a feast for them. Paneer, mutton, Kashmiri pulao, dahi balla, kebabs, chhole and puris. At the last moment your mother panicked because she thought the food may be too north Indian for their taste. So I made some sambar and curd rice for them. But they preferred our food. Who can blame them? They put coconut and tamarind in all their dishes.'

I think it best to leave her to her culinary reminiscences and head back to my room, carrying a mass of confusion in my head.

I call up Vrinda. There is one thing to be said in her favour. She never ignores my calls. I get straight to the point. 'Did you visit my mother a few months before she died?'

There is silence at the other end followed by a dry laugh. 'Don't tell me I am a suspect too?'

'I just want to know what prompted you to make a trip all the way from Coimbatore to Lucknow.'

'Business.' She decides it's best to be matter-of-fact about the whole thing. 'We wanted to expand and turn into a corporate entity with a pan-India branding rather than confine ourselves to the south. And Randeep felt Lucknow as the second largest city in central and northern India, was a better bet to invest in than Delhi and Gurgaon that have so many players. Didn't your source tell you Randeep had accompanied me too?'

'So it was a social visit. How come no one thought it fit to inform me that you were visiting my mother in Lucknow?'

'Relax, Neha. It was a little more than a social visit. There was a business element to it. A new SEZ was coming up in Lucknow and Randeep felt it might be worthwhile checking out whether our software company that has its corporate headquarters in UK can operate from there.'

'How could Mother help you with all that?' I don't want to sound overtly suspicious but given what Vrinda is saying, I can't help it.

'Not your mother,' she hesitates a bit before continuing. 'But you do know how influential your father is in political circles in UP?'

I am so angry that I fear that I might smash the phone I am holding. I try to keep my voice steady when I accuse her: 'So all this business networking was going on behind my back; you were using my mother and I was kept in the dark about it?'

When she responds after a split second, her voice is cool and distant. 'No one was using your mother. She charged for these meetings and we were more than willing to pay her the usual commission. In fact, I tried my best not to let her know it was my organization she was dealing with. She only came to know when we met at her place. The way these things work, we had got in touch with her through another man who works these deals from Chennai and I had specifically asked him to keep our identities secret. We didn't want Samir and you involved in any way. Once we met, she was extremely embarrassed and stubbornly refused to take any payment from us.' She pauses once again before concluding, 'I told you all this has nothing to do with her murder. This is how we work when we have to do business with any government body. There may be a lot of talk about globalization but nothing can do away with the corruption that is inherent to us.'

I am not sure what stings me more. The condemnation of my parents or the curt manner in which she has stated it. I am not surprised at how closely my sanctimonious tone of disapproval echoes hers.

'And I am sure corporate entities need take no responsibility for their contribution in this entire mess. Bribing is not as big a crime as getting bribed...'

'I was not saying we are not to blame. Now if you don't mind, I have to prepare for a conference tomorrow,' she says tiredly and hangs up.

I find it difficult to sleep after this conversation. It has shed light on many of the unanswered questions I have been dealing with after Mother's death. Starting with the large financial legacy my mother has left for me. As a child I hated the dinners Mother threw at home for perfect strangers. When I grew older I turned even more resentful towards them as I thought the visitors were important contacts for the man to cultivate. I believed he was using her to further his political interests. He was the corrupt one and my mother always the victim in my eyes. Not that I ever forgave her for settling into the victim mode so easily.

Thanks to Vrinda I have a totally new perspective on my parents. Neither of them seems to have been particularly wronged in their relationship with each other. Both of them extracted what they could.

Curiously enough I also start to feel the nervousness I should have felt for my mother when she was alive. It is apparent now that she must have had her share of enemies. Disgruntled business barons who couldn't get what they wanted because the price demanded was too high, rival brokers and middlemen who had access to other powerful politicians and resented Mother's success, maybe other politicians who wanted her for themselves.

If it wasn't for a woman who was murdered in another part of the country in exactly the same manner as Mother, I would have believed that her murderer belonged to Lucknow. Battling his demons in the night just the way I am battling mine.

Samir may have had nothing to do with Mother's murder. After all he hates the family business as much as I hated Mother's family connections.

They bloom for lovers

Mother bought me clothes that I never touched. She wanted me to wear bright colours. I hated the dresses she got for me but she never gave up. It was all girlie stuff picked up from designer boutiques.

She was partial to wearing saris and ethnic outfits designed by a retired filmmaker who lived in Lucknow and specialized in chikan work. Every time she went to him to buy something for herself, she picked up something for me. These have accumulated in a shelf of her cupboard. I try them on one by one. I also try on some of her jewellery that is in the house. I know most of her gold and diamonds are safe in a bank locker but she kept some at home, things she used more frequently: tiny ear-studs with glittering diamonds and rubies on them; the rings, which she wore on all her fingers; gold bangles and necklaces. I examine myself closely in the mirror after dressing up in the clothes I never looked at when she was alive, and the jewellery I dismissed as being tacky. I can never look like her but I have to admit they make me appear more feminine; softer somehow.

Jamuna knocks on the door and when she sees me dressed like a film-star from the sixties in a turquoise salwar kameez with exquisite embroidery and tiny gold danglers in my ears, her eyes widen in amazement.

'You should start thinking of getting married,' she advises.

I start to laugh and then check myself when I notice how serious she is. 'Why do you want me to get married?' I ask her.

'So that you don't end up like her. She had everything except a proper husband,' she says wistfully. 'If she had one, he would have stayed with her and protected her.'

She has come to the room to fetch the detergent that was always kept in a shelf in mother's bathroom. She is holding on to the past in whatever way she can. She doesn't look at me when she leaves the room with the packet.

I turn to the mirror again. I have been confused about how I should confront Samir when I meet him next. Now I know words won't be necessary. Dressed like this, I look like her ghost. It will be enough to disarm him and make him share with me what he has been concealing all along.

Ideally I should have just gone to Coimbatore. After all, that's where Vrinda claims her precious son is recuperating. But I know going there is futile. With all the power and influence she wields in that city, I am likely to get stonewalled at every step. I think it best to leave for Coonoor instead and wait there for Samir to show up. Deep down I know I am lying even to myself. It's her and Kabir I want to meet. But I console myself saying that I want to meet her for a particular reason. After all, she lived with him just before he came to Lucknow and Mother was murdered. She is bound to have some knowledge that can help me.

I check into the hotel next to the old church, close to Samir's cottage. There is nowhere else I can stay anyway. You need a member to check you into the club and I don't want Vrinda to know I am back. Not as yet, anyway.

The woman at the reception looks puzzled when I tell her that I don't know how long I will stay. She relaxes only when I pay the advance for two days in cash. They are used to having holiday visitors usually over the weekends. No one stays long term. I can afford to stay on for as long as I want to. But once I am ensconced in the luxurious room, I have no idea what to do next. I would much rather rent a cottage for myself. Hotels always make me feel as if all my moves are being closely monitored. I am not sure whether there are houses that are rented out in this town. But I need to shift to a place of my own. Just like Sujala and Kabir did, starting out in the hotel, and then finding the ideal home for themselves.

I decide Mrs Kashyap will be my best bet if I need to find a place to stay longer. She would also know if anyone has been to Samir's cottage after I left for Delhi. After lunch I make my way to her cottage. The sun is out and she is in her garden tending her plants. She looks up when she sees me opening the gate. It takes her a while to recognize me. Either she is short-sighted or she has a failing memory. Considering her age either is a possibility.

She confesses she has forgotten my name as she leads me inside. She also mentions I look different. I am still wearing jeans but the sweater I have on is something Mother got me when she had gone to Europe with the man three years ago. I am also wearing a touch of make-up and her perfume. I may not be transformed, but I do carry the promise. I feel unreasonably happy that Mrs Kashyap has noticed the change.

'Why have you come back?' she comes to the point without much ado.

I tell her I want to live in Coonoor for some time.

She looks puzzled. 'But no one lives here except old retired folks like me. The rest use their cottages as holiday retreats.'

'Samir lived here,' I insist stubbornly.

'He is an artist. Besides, his wealthy mother can support him. I thought you worked in Delhi?'

'My mother died. She left me some money. I want to invest in a property here. I can only do that if I stay here for a while. For that I need to rent a place.'

'I don't take PGs,' she says flatly.

'I wasn't hoping to stay here,' I tell her hurriedly. 'I would prefer something independent.'

She frowns. 'I am not sure whether it is safe. Ever since Karla was killed like that...'

'You stay alone and nothing has happened to you,' I respond brightly.

'I have a woman who comes in the evening to prepare dinner for me and then she stays the night.'

'Maybe I can do the same. I am sure I can get someone to stay with me. I can't cook to save my life,' I tell her.

She starts to smile on hearing this and then she looks away. 'You young people are so reckless. No proper guidance. Our generation was different. We knew at every stage of life what needed to be done. There was a time to study and a time to get married. After we got married, the children came and once they were grown up enough to go to school, we had to look for a suitable job for a woman that could supplement the husband's income. Like that of a teacher. Or tutoring from home. There was no confusion.'

'I have always been confused. My mother never followed any traditions. She was content being the mistress of a wealthy man,' I blurt out before I can stop myself.

She looks startled at first and then smiles kindly. 'That couldn't have been out of choice. Poor thing. There must have been compelling reasons for her to agree to an arrangement like that.'

Neither of us have the words to carry the conversation forward but the silence that comes to rest between us is comfortable.

'I will check with some of the other ladies I know in town if any place is up for rent. Also my maid. They are usually much more in the know about what is happening. Do you have a budget? How much rent are you willing to pay?'

She nods her head in exasperation when I tell her that I haven't thought of a figure. 'How typical of your generation. You just don't know the value of money.'

I decide to leave before she starts on another sermon.

Shrinks like Kalpana will tell you there is nothing like coincidence. The pull of your psyche takes you to places where the unconscious guides you. Nothing is an accident in life. You meet somebody because you want to, not because you run into this person accidentally. So when I spot her in front of the church as I am taking a walk the next morning after a late breakfast I am not surprised. I had intended to walk by her cottage hoping one of them would spot me and call me inside. I didn't think of what would happen next but it wasn't important. I just had to meet her and feel the excitement of being in her company.

Lost in her thoughts, she doesn't notice me until my shadow falls on her. She looks up and smiles tentatively at me, one hand over her forehead, trying to shield her eyes from the sun.

'It's you. I have thought about you a lot in the past few days,' she says lowering her hand as well as her head. I shock myself with a realization. I can finally acknowledge to myself something I have been running away from all along. I am in love with her.

Samir had told me about a girl from our class who had gone to the US and become a lesbian. He had met her with her partner in New York in a night club and had brought back a picture of the two of them for me. We had giggled over it. Same sex love was something that happened to other people. The ones we spot on television sometime; men who wear make-up and women who refuse to do their upper lip. There is a lot of talk about stereotyping them to discriminate against them. Activists are always trying to tell you that sexuality is a matter of choice and you cannot tell by just looking at someone which way a person swings. But the representatives I spot in magazine articles and on television channels seem to wear their uniqueness on their sleeve. That may have been the reason why Samir and I had been so shocked and perversely titillated by our classmate Tarla's transformation. She had been a quiet girl, doing very well in studies. We had thought of her as a nerd and someone who was completely asexual even though she was pretty.

Samir had asked me whether she had hit on any of the girls in the dorm. He had also teased me cruelly by saying she was most likely to have made a pass at me since I had so many dyke-like characteristics. It was another of his jibes that had hurt a lot at that time but I had taken care to hide my pain from him.

I guess like most straight people who want the world to believe they are politically correct I have also made noises in public about how there is nothing wrong or shocking about falling in love with someone of the same gender. I brought in Tarla only to share how different we are when it comes to talking about the same thing with those whom we feel we can trust. We roll our eyes, we want to gossip about it.

Owning up to my feelings has shocked me to my core. I find I am unable to speak. When she gestures to me to sit beside her, I do as I am told. I have lost my ability to think. A kind of numbness, like a dark cloud, takes over. I want her to go on talking without looking at me because I am not sure what she will read in my face.

But she seems to be even more preoccupied than I am. Even though she is talking to me as she sits by my side, her attention is elsewhere. I don't mind so long as I can feel her presence. She points out to the Kurinji shrubs that divide the graveyard from the church. 'They are so beautiful,' she says dreamily. 'I find it so fascinating that they bloom only once in twelve years.'

'They are meant to be divine. I am not sure of this, but

I remember a girl in my school telling me that they are offered to Muruga.'

'There is a god called Muruga? I didn't know that.'

'He is known as Muruga in the south. In the north he is more popular as Karthik, Ganesh's brother. The lesser-known son of Shiva and Parvathi.'

'I don't know about Karthik either. But my mother worshipped Shiva. I know that. Since she was the only religious one in the family and died when I was eight, I am afraid I grew up without much knowledge about Hindu gods and goddesses.'

I warm to her confidences. I have always considered myself to be a psychological orphan. We have things in common now. As if reading my thoughts, she continues: 'My father married again. An American. She wasn't religious either.'

'Where did you live as a child?' I ask.

'Lincoln, Nebraska. My father and his brother migrated there from their village in UP. The typical Indian immigrant story. They had an uncle there who owned a couple of motels. He needed cheap labour. They started with him, worked hard. Expanded. Now my entire extended family owns motels, gas stations and Indian grocery stores across the midwest.'

She is telling me things she has not shared with anyone else in the town. We are forging a connection and it makes me very happy.

She turns to me. 'Why are they offered to this god?'

'I don't know. All I know is that he is a bachelor god and Kurinji is a flower meant for lovers,' I blush when I say this.

She starts to laugh and then turns serious again, clearly distracted by something else. 'I want Samir to come back. It is not as if *he* doesn't care but *he* was so much more with me when Samir was around. If only Samir could understand,' she says slowly.

I don't know whether it is my state of mind or what she is saying, but it all sounds jumbled to me. Not that I care. It is enough for me that I am sitting beside her.

'Let's go and meet him,' she announces as she gets up and oddly enough starts walking in the opposite direction to where she lives. I wonder what Kabir is doing there. It is only when we are near Samir's cottage that I realize my blunder. She thinks Samir is back and I am staying with him.

'Wait,' I tell her as she looks impatiently at me, waiting for me to open the locked gate. 'Samir is not here. And I am not staying here either.'

'Oh,' she says. 'Where is he?'

'I have no idea. I called up Vrinda from Delhi a couple of times and she said he hasn't recovered. The last time I called her from Lucknow we didn't talk about him at all.'

She is looking confused now. 'Who did you think we were going to meet?' she asks frowning.

'I thought you meant Kabir,' I say in a small voice.

She smiles and I feel the sun on my face. 'Let's go then. I am sure Kabir would like to hear what you have been up to after leaving here.'

Six legs intertwined

The strain is evident in Kabir's face when he opens the door for us. His eyes travel from his wife to me standing just behind her. He smiles tentatively and makes way for both of us to enter. It is clear from the apron he wears over his T-shirt that he has been in the kitchen making lunch.

'Neha wanted to meet you,' Sujala says perfunctorily and flops down on the large sofa. I don't know how to respond to that. I hadn't told her I wanted to meet Kabir; the whole thing had arisen out of the confusion over Samir. But I don't know how to explain it. Thankfully, Kabir takes her at her word.

'Of course,' he says, waving me to a chair. 'I am so happy to meet you again. You will stay for lunch, won't you?'

I nod brightly at him. There is nothing else I can say or do anyway.

'I am cooking Chinese today. Noodles and steamed rice with vegetables. I hope you are fine with that.'

'I love Chinese,' I tell him. Truth is, I have no particular fondness for any one type of cuisine. I can eat anything that's cooked so long as it's not burnt or stale.

'That's good to know,' this time his smile is a lot warmer. He goes back into the kitchen. Sujala is leaning back on the sofa, her eyes shut. She opens them slowly and looks at me.

'Stop. You are staring at me,' she accuses sitting up stiffly.

I feel a flush creep up my neck. I don't want her to know what I feel for her. She might be revolted and throw me out of her house. She might never want to see me again. The thought is unbearable.

'Relax,' she laughs. 'I didn't mean it like that. It's quite flattering actually.'

I look away. The fierce jealous passion I experience belongs to someone much younger. It would be fitting for a schoolgirl who develops a crush on her senior. Not someone who until a few weeks ago prided herself as a management professional. I used to think emotions were a sign of weakness – something that women who wanted to make a mark in organizations should always avoid.

She gets up from the sofa to go to the kitchen. 'I better check if Kabir needs some help.' She pauses by my chair and gently touches me on one of my cheeks. I get goose-bumps. Her hand seems to contain fragrant mysteries that can belong only to fairy tales. I know now she understands. I am not the first woman to react to her like this. I am filled with an inexplicable dread.

The dining room is rather American, an extension of the kitchen separated by a wooden counter. Kabir has opened a bottle of wine in my honour. The meal he has cooked is delicious, a mushroom and bamboo shoot soup that he has made with fresh ingredients and not from a tin; crisp noodles with shreds of pork in them and rice with steamed leafy vegetables and spring onions. There is a side dish of boneless chicken with sesame seeds. I have prided myself all along about being oblivious to the lure of food. But now I know why people turn into foodies.

There is hardly any conversation when we are eating. All of us concentrate on the food. The bottle of wine lasts only as long as the meal. Sujala leans back and reaches for a pack of cigarettes placed on top of the sideboard, next to the dining table.

'I hope you don't mind,' she says as she lights up.

'Actually I don't mind having one,' I tell her. She extends the pack to me.

'I am trying to give up,' Sujala says.

'You have been trying to give up for the last two years,' Kabir interjects. 'I find smoking disgusting,' he says turning to me and laughing.

'I did give up when we came here because you hated it,' Sujala protests. 'I started smoking only after you left.'

He gives her a warning look that doesn't escape me. I feel embarrassed. I am the intruder here. They should have the freedom to say what they want to in their own house.

'Do you smoke regularly?' Kabir asks me to change the subject.

'I hardly smoke,' I tell him. It is true. There was a time in school when I smoked a lot. Samir and I would sneak out into the large grounds on the pretext of taking a walk and go behind the trees. We were never caught. But then they did not catch us even on the day of the school feast, when I was losing my virginity to him. I am not sure whether it would be sensible to mention Samir at a time when all of us are so happy so I stop at the denial.

'There is some ice cream in case you want dessert,' Kabir offers.

'I am too full. As it is I am having trouble keeping awake. Wine in the afternoon always makes me sleepy.'

They send me to the living room despite my protests that I would like to help, while they clear the table and wash up.

I take the sofa this time and sink into it. The cigarette has done nothing to prevent the drowsiness from taking over. I am unable to stop my eyes from closing. I curl up and go to sleep.

I wake to find a rug over me and a pillow under my head. I have no idea how long I have been asleep. The large grandfather clock on the wall says twenty minutes past three but I didn't check the time when I came back to the room after lunch. I look around. Neither of them is present. Perhaps they are taking a nap too. I realize how thirsty I am and walk towards the kitchen. I can't spot a jug of water either on the dining table or on the kitchen counter. I realize the tap with the sink is attached to a water filter. I pick up a glass and place it under the tap and drink thirstily. Too much of wine has dehydrated me. My head feels heavy.

As I am leaving the kitchen I notice a stairway. I walk towards it mesmerized. There is a room facing the stairway. I peep in. It has the unlived look that guest rooms have. I take the stairs. The large master bedroom is to the right and the door to the room is wide open.

I can see her riding him. Neither of them is wearing any clothes. I stand by the door. It is as if I have been transported to a cinema to watch an explicit love-making scene from a European film where the actors are uninhibited and nothing appears vulgar. He has his eyes shut as his hands travel all over her body coming to rest on her breasts time and again. He whispers something I cannot hear and she opens her eyes and looks at him. From where I am I can see one of her erect nipples. Suddenly she moans loudly and he turns his head and spots me. His eyes widen and he looks away blushing.

I draw back involuntarily with a startled sigh. She turns and spots me at that moment. He quietly removes himself from beneath her and throws a dressing-gown over his taut glistening body and slips into what I presume to be the bathroom.

Sujala continues to stare at me then lies back in the same mound that Kabir made in the bed when she was making love to him. Her dark brown hair frames one half of her face as she turns and beckons to me.

'Come,' she says.

I walk to the large four poster bed and stand looking at her. She takes my hand impatiently and pulls me beside her.

'Make love to me as only a woman can,' she whispers sitting up. Her hands reach out to yank the sweater off me. I feel ashamed about my ignorance. For the first time a woman is undressing me in bed, gently biting my earlobes, her tongue travelling all over my neck, her fingers gently squeezing my nipples and all I can do is to sit there feeling terribly inexperienced. I want to pre-empt all her desires and be a slave to all her bidding but I am the novice here. She is a good teacher. Soon our bodies are entwined.

I know Kabir can hear us from the bathroom and I don't know how to stop. I am on all fours now bending and kissing her all over as she moans in pleasure. Sometime in the midst of our love-making I hear a sound and look up to see a fully-clothed Kabir staring at us from near the door. There is nothing in his face to tell me what he is thinking. I cannot stop my hands and lips travelling all over her body. They are beyond my control. I smile at him uncertainly as Sujala moans again. He walks out of the room without turning back.

I don't how long we lie in each other's arms afterwards while her husband waits outside. She is the first to wriggle out from my arms and go into the bathroom. She comes out after a while with a towel around her. She flings it on the bed as I lie on the bed watching her put on her clothes. Fully dressed, she comes and sits on the bed and kisses me on my mouth.

'Get up,' she says. 'Kabir must be waiting with the tea.'

All the time I was making love to her, it hadn't occurred to me that there is going to be an afterwards. But when I am in the bathroom debating whether I should wash or just let all her smells stay with me, I wonder what awaits me when I meet Kabir again.

I shouldn't have worried. They are both in the living room, sitting on the sofa, facing each other, looking outside the window. A tray with a steaming kettle and three cups is on the centre table.

'It rained in the afternoon,' Kabir remarks as I stand near the door uncertainly.

'How do you like your tea? Light or strong?' she checks before reaching out for the pot.

They accompany me to the hotel afterwards. Sujala and me walking together, talking and giggling while Kabir walks a little distance away from us. He is looking older somehow. We can be his wards and he the designated chaperone to keep an eye on us. The walk for some strange reason evokes a sense of déjà vu in me although this is the first time I am out with both of them.

'How long are you intending to stay? I quite liked the hotel when we first came and stayed here,' she says as we near the gate.

'I am booked until noon tomorrow. I am going to extend it by a week. I hope to find a more permanent place by then.'

'Why don't you move in with us?' asks Kabir in a quiet voice as I turn to him surprised.

'Actually that's a good idea,' Sujala says. 'In any case, it's not as if you know anyone else here, apart from Samir, and we don't know whether he is ever coming back.'

I haven't thought of Samir or my mother the entire afternoon. Being with her helps me blank out everything else I need to live with.

As I stand there, hesitating, Kabir makes up my mind for me. 'We will send a cab for you around noon tomorrow. You can check out and come home straight.'

I nod, smiling at both of them. 'Thank you,' I murmur quite overcome. 'Why don't you guys have dinner with me in the hotel?'

'No thanks,' she says. 'I don't think I am up to it tonight. The afternoon has tired me. I want to sleep early. You take care.' She kisses me on my cheek and turns to go.

Kabir puts his arms around her waist as she leans against his shoulder. They start walking. Kabir looks back after sometime to wave at me. She doesn't. I can kill him.

Now I know what induces the rage in a person that can lead to murder.

Days of leisure

One year, the man decided to celebrate his birthday with us. There must have been a catch. Maybe his legitimate family was out of town. Maybe he sent them away to be with my nagging mother. Maybe guilt finally caught up with him that year. All I can remember about that day was that it was one of the worst of my life. A few of his friends came over, minus their wives, of course. I am sure they allowed their spouses to accompany them only when they were visiting his family home that housed his overweight wife and his needy children. There was just one other woman present apart from my mother. She smoked a lot and had a loud laugh.

I stayed in my room with Jamuna as both of us were instructed to. Mother peeped in to call us out only when it was time for the man to cut the cake. It was a horrible strawberry coloured confection that one of his flunkeys had brought him. They lit the single candle on it, which he then blew out to the sound of loud claps and a ghastly rendition of happy birthday. I must have been about eleven or twelve and was terribly embarrassed at the way my mother was behaving. She was behaving like a giddy-headed teenager, standing next to the man and giggling at the photographer and imploring him to click more pictures. Suddenly she picked up a small piece of cake and forced it into the man's reluctant mouth, gesturing to the photographer to capture the moment.

By that time I was clinging to Jamuna's hand, a little frightened by the smoke-filled room and the smell of alcohol. We retreated behind two safari-suit clad men. I heard one of them whispering to his companion: '*Saali randi ke naatak to dekh...*' I was old enough to understand that he was talking about my mother in a derogatory way. But more than me, it was Jamuna who was outraged by this and she almost dragged me back to my room muttering curses under her breath.

I have always tried to push away the memory of that evening. It comes back again as I stand splashing water on my face in the hotel bathroom. I don't flinch this time. I tell myself I have finally owned up to my dubious legacy.

I thought I had been in love earlier. Till just a few days ago, because of the complex feelings I harboured for Samir, I wasn't sure whether I continued to carry a torch for Samir long after our apology of an affair had ended when we were still at school. So I am sure most rational souls will tell me that I am infatuated with her. Except I know that isn't true. I love her with my entire being. I have never loved anyone like this. If I was given a choice to replay one moment from the past I know I would choose the afternoon we made love. I tell myself that this is something so precious that having discovered it I am going to make it last a lifetime.

There is Kabir, and she seems to care for him, but he won't last. We will be together, she and I, and we'll grow old in that cottage together. I have been running all my life and, finally, I am home with her. He has left her once before and he will leave her again. A little voice interrupts to tell me that I am making the same mistake that Samir did. But I stifle it. Samir was like a little child. He needed to be taken care of all the time. Anyone would tire of him. But that won't happen with us. We sense each other's longings much before they dress themselves in words.

I get up a million times in the night because all the tossing and turning in bed cannot lull me to sleep. I stand near the window and look for the moon in the sky. I pour myself many glasses of water, some of which I drink and some of which I empty in the basin.

I cannot wait for morning. And then I count the hours to noon.

I am no longer concerned about the murder of my mother. I tell myself that the truth about it will emerge when the time is right.

I cannot be distracted. I have this one chance of discovering the real thing and cannot blow it. This kind of love is not selfless. It is all needs and desires.

When I finally fall asleep in the early hours of dawn I have the same dream about her. *We get into Samir's cottage together. She leaves me sitting on the sofa and goes inside Samir's room. He comes out dragging her body behind him...* This time I scream and wake up. I am sweating all over.

The sun is out and this brings a sense of pragmatism about me. I tell myself I didn't come back all the way just to get into a messy relationship. My reasons for coming back are to confront Samir and elicit a confession from him. I cannot let her come between me and my goal.

I call room service and ask them to send breakfast to my room. A woman calls shortly afterward from the front office to find out whether I am checking out today. I inform her I am planning to move out by noon but it is likely I may come back after a day or two and the hotel may have to accommodate me again. She tells me the best way to ensure that a room's kept ready is to book it in advance.

I have not checked with the hotel about room availability because I think the two of them will wake up in the morning and decide to withdraw the invitation. What I am unsure about is how long I will last in that house. It is not as if I have got her out of my system. I am sure all it will take is one meeting for me to thaw towards her again. I find her irresistible, but I am hoping once I start staying with them I will be able to discover some chinks in her armour. There are so many unanswered questions in my mind. Like, why is her husband so tolerant of her sexual dalliances? Why have they invited me to stay with them when they barely know me? Was there an agenda behind what happened between the two of us yesterday in the afternoon?

There is something about the two of them that doesn't fit. They have behaved strangely all along. After all, if Samir was Karla's killer then surely Sujala knows she was the catalyst that fuelled his rage. And even if she is in denial of this, she is aware of the bare facts – that her friend Karla, who not so long ago gave her a job, has been brutally murdered. She didn't know my mother but she must have been fond of Karla. How come she has never brought her up in our conversations about Samir? If I had a friend who was killed like that I would think of her every time someone brought up the name of the person the police suspected had murdered her.

I wonder whether I am trying too hard to prove to myself that I can be objective about her. I have never seen my mood swing to such extremes. I am happy as long as I think of having her in my life; I am miserable when I am reminded of all that I would have to put at stake to go on loving her.

I tell myself that, for the time being, all I need to do is to keep my thoughts in abeyance and wait for the taxi they have promised to send for me.

Kabir opens the door and shows me to the guest room. He informs me Sujala is in bed as she is not feeling too well and will come down in an hour or so. I want to see her immediately of course but I don't know how I can do that. Yesterday seems to have been forgotten. It's not as if Kabir is behaving differently today. He is warm and polite as always. Just that he doesn't seem to remember that he saw his wife making love to me less than twenty-four hours ago. Maybe this is the way he copes. His behaviour would have made more sense if he had indicated his anger; instead he is completely at ease with me.

I change out of my jeans and sweater for lunch. I wear one of the dresses Mother had bought for me. It is a lilac-coloured ensemble. I put a dash of kohl on my eyes and brush my lips with pale pink lipstick. I know I look attractive but, curiously, instead of feeling confident I feel more uncertain. I have no idea how she will react when she sees me like this. If she mocks me I will die of embarrassment.

I shouldn't have worried. When she comes down for lunch, snivelling and blowing her nose, her eyes watering, all she can manage is a weak smile. I don't think my new look registers with either of them.

'I am sorry,' she says. 'I am extremely prone to colds here, in India.'

The lunch Kabir has prepared today is in keeping with his wife's ailment. There is a peppery chicken soup followed by steaming rice, dal and vegetables.

'Always feed a cold,' he urges his wife piling her plate with food while she protests. I want to go and cuddle her like Mother used to when I fell ill during the holidays. But today there is no space for me in the intimacy they two seem to share. I have no idea what I am doing in this house with them.

Sujala goes back to her room as soon as we finish lunch. The conversation has been desultory. I help Kabir stack the dishes in the dishwasher. I ask him whether they have ever considered getting a part-time help to assist with their domestic chores. 'No, we are strictly against that kind of a thing. Both of us think it is very exploitative.'

'It does give them income and opportunities they won't have otherwise,' I protest feebly, thinking of Jamuna.

'No doubt that's how they looked at slavery in the US, once upon a time,' he says with a dry laugh.

Sujala recovers in a couple of days, then Kabir catches the cold from her, and now it is my turn; so each of us spends a couple of days with the virus. A runny nose is no aphrodisiac but that afternoon is never far from my mind. When we are together I have eyes only for her. I notice the smallest of things – the way her lips curl crookedly when she smiles, how her eyes turn distant when she gets irritated and annoyed, how thin her fingers are, how long her eyelashes.

They treat me differently. Kabir is a lot more indulgent with me, like I am a child who has been entrusted to his care. But she can get impatient. She snaps when she is irritable. She is much more prone to contradict me when I am airing my opinions. There are long spells when she withdraws into herself. I don't mind. I have felt at home after years, in this cottage with the two of them. I am just content to be.

It is like a long, extended holiday. We wake up around nine every day and have breakfast around ten. Afterwards we take turns to read the papers. Kabir does some work on his computer. I learn he is a professor with tenure in the university and is on a long sabbatical to write a book. He doesn't tell me what it is about. Sujala does the laundry and cleaning while I make preparations for lunch. I do all the chopping and grinding for Kabir to come in later and cook. Around half past noon, Kabir comes into the kitchen. I learn soon enough how fastidious he is. He likes to keep the kitchen spotlessly clean. In that respect I am a good helper for him to have. The long years in the hostel have ingrained neatness in me. Like him, I too, like order and structure, and ensure everything is kept the way he likes it.

Some evenings we smoke weed. There seems to be a never-ending supply of it in the house. They say it reacts differently with different folks. All I can say is it just paralyses me and stops me from thinking. Other evenings we sit around and read or play Scrabble and Pictionary. There is always music playing in the background. Kabir is partial to western classical, especially Wagner. He also listens to Urdu ghazals, Begum Akhtar and Abida Parveen. Sujala is fond of retro stuff like me. Both of us love Simon and Garfunkel.

There is no talk of sex. If the two of them are doing it they are taking care to ensure that I don't get to hear about it. I have reached out to her once or twice but she has rebuffed my advances, taking care not to offend me. I may as well be visiting cousins – not that I have ever known any. None of it actually matters. I am content just being in her presence.

We go out for a walk every afternoon, which is when the two of us do all our sharing. I talk about being in school and how isolated I felt all through college because Samir went away to Paris to study art; about my two-year stint at a management institute followed by my job in Delhi; about how Mother and I could never agree on anything when she was alive; about what Samir has meant to me in all these years and the sense of betrayal I am living with when it comes to him.

She shares with me her childhood spent in Lincoln, Nebraska, with her father and an aloof stepmother who has a daughter of her own. 'There is just a difference of a year between my stepsister Joanne and me, and we are very close. She is in Sydney, Australia, working for a non-government organization. She is the only one in the family who understood.'

'Understood what?' I ask, unable to prevent myself even though I know all information about her past has to be volunteered by her. She is uncomfortable with questions.

Kabir butts in just then to say it looks like it is going to rain and we should head back.

I spot Mrs Kashyap on our way back. She is hurrying too, looking at the sky. I am sure she sees the three of us but when I wave out to her cheerfully, she looks away. I try to explain. 'She is so old. Perhaps she didn't recognize me.'

Kabir laughs dryly. 'More likely the dragon living next door has informed her that you are staying with us. You are a pariah now.'

'I have to go and meet her one of these days. She promised to look for a place for me,' I protest feebly.

It is the first time I have brought up the topic of moving out. Neither of them react to what I have just said. I feel wretched. She could have said there is no question of me making a home away from her. Instead her eyes are opaque and her mouth is set in a grim determined line. As if seeing Mrs Kashyap has spoilt the day for her.

It's too good to last. This idyllic existence I have with the two of them. I try very hard to dislike Kabir but find it impossible. I have these bouts of jealousy but when he is with me he comes across as being so caring that I feel I can depend much more on him than her. Sometimes she withdraws completely, making me feel that the only reason I am still staying in the cottage is because Kabir wants me to. I am aware she is toying with me except I don't know what she is getting out of it.

As if it is time to burst the bubble, when I wake up late the next morning, the world has gone haywire.

And leave me all alone

Kabir informs me at the breakfast table that they have to go back to the US immediately and he doesn't know how long they will be away. She sits impassively, smoking a cigarette and taking care not to look at me while he is talking.

'A very dear friend of ours has been diagnosed with a serious ailment. It was detected late. The doctors are not optimistic.'

'When did you find out?' I ask, my heart thudding madly.

'This morning... when I checked my mail. After a pause he adds, 'You can stay on in the cottage as long as you want. Until you are ready to go back.'

'Go back where?' I am finding it difficult to be as practical as him in the circumstances.

'For god's sake, Neha, does everything have to be about you? Samir was the same,' she turns to Kabir with a frown, stubbing out her cigarette. 'I guess it's about being brought up in this country.' She gets up and announces she has to pack and leaves the room.

I would have found it more bearable if she had slapped me. I blink back my tears as Kabir comes from behind me to take my plate. He pats me gently on the shoulder. 'You are going to be fine without us.'

I nod and go back to my room without offering to help him with the dishes. I think I will cry once I am back in my room but, strangely enough, I cannot muster any tears. Instead all I can do is sit like a dummy and stare into space.

It is always a shock when you encounter cruelty for the first time from someone you don't associate it with. Not because you think the person is incapable of it but because you have imagined things are so perfect between the two of you that the object of your affection can never show that side to you. Once you get over the initial reaction, other emotions take over. You get angry with that person. You want to show you don't care. You have to prove to the world that the snub didn't matter to you and it's the person's loss and not yours that things didn't work out.

I would no doubt have sulked with her if they weren't leaving. But since my feelings of outrage are mixed with grief at her departure I don't quite know what to do; how to react. I just sit there until Kabir knocks at the door to tell me the taxi has come to fetch them.

I go out trying hard to smile. She kisses me frostily on my cheek before walking out of the door pulling her bag. Kabir hugs me and follows her. He turns to wave to me as soon as the taxi starts moving. She is bent on punishing me so she doesn't turn back.

I go back to my room and lie down on my bed and the tears that have shown such commendable restraint since morning flow like a tap.

Life is not worth living without her. I skip lunch and find the strength to get up from bed only when it starts to get dark. I make myself some coffee and spy her pack of cigarettes lying on the dining table. She has forgotten to take them with her. There are four left in the pack. I smoke all four one after the other. Sitting there I have a panic attack when I realize they have not given me their address in the US. I haven't noticed either of them carrying a cellphone. There is a landline connection in the house but I have not seen either of them making or receiving calls. I gingerly lift the receiver. The buzz of the dial tone tells me it is working. And then I find my heart sink once again when it occurs to me that the phone is something they must have inherited from the previous owner, like everything else in the house. They may not have even stored the number. We have not even exchanged email ids – you don't need to mail those you are living with.

After a miserable night, I wake up at noon to a fresh resolution. I am going to be strong and not behave like a little child. I decide I will find a way to keep myself busy until they return. I am going to start by cleaning the cottage. Deep down I know the cleaning is an excuse. I want to go to their room and search for something – anything – that will give me a clue about where they are. I have gathered from past conversations that Sujala is from Lincoln, Nebraska. Does that hold true for Kabir as well? They have always stonewalled me whenever I have tried to find out anything about their past.

I try to push away all the memories of the one afternoon I have spent in the room and look around. Nothing except her presence had registered the first time. Now my eyes take in the large four poster bed and the two large wooden cupboards arranged side by side near the wall opposite the bed. The left side of the room is taken up by a wooden writing table with a straight-backed chair. A printer sits on it that is no doubt connected to Kabir's laptop except he has taken it with him. A wooden rocking chair placed next to the bed is the only other piece of furniture. I move to the table where I spy a sheaf of papers. They are printed and Kabir has scrawled all over them. He was probably proof-reading them before he left.

I sit on the chair and go through them. It is clear that the book he is writing has something to do with alternative sexualities in the subcontinent. There are references to practices followed by trans-genders in rural India. Another section consists of lesbian case studies in India, Pakistan and Bangladesh. I find myself going red in the face. Is this what I meant to them all along? Some kind of guinea pig for the book he was writing? Does he take me to be a full-fledged dyke? I have never felt so humiliated in my life. Behind the gentle veneer is a shrewd man who has been using me all along.

I try the drawers of the table and find more printed papers inside. Frustrated, I bang them shut and sit there feeling cold and miserable. I had come to the room with a vacuum cleaner. That was the excuse I had been making to myself but now I know I needn't have bothered. The discovery of Kabir's research justifies my prying.

They have been using me. I have every right to find out about them.

Before leaving the room, I decide to search the drawers once again. I take out the papers to see if there is anything at the bottom. Some photographs that seem to have inadvertently got mixed up with them slide out. I pick them up. The first photograph is of a protest march. The protestors carry banners that say 'Stop Hate Crimes' and 'Justice for Brandon Teena and Matthew Shepard'. I look at it more carefully but neither of them is in the picture. The second photograph is of Kabir, dressed in jeans and a sweatshirt that says 'University of Nebraska', participating in the same march and holding a banner along with a tall, elegant-looking woman. The next one is taken in a living room. It has the same woman sitting on Kabir's lap. Sujala sits next to them, smiling. A young, good-looking man with a glass of wine in his hand stands behind the sofa. He is smiling too. It is obvious that they have all posed for the picture after having set the camera. The last one has the three of them having a meal together without the young man. He must have taken the picture. Kabir's attire seems to indicate that the pictures were taken on the same day as the march. I put the photographs back in the drawer and go downstairs.

Suspicions I have pushed to the back of my mind start to resurface. There is something decidedly odd about the way they abruptly abandoned their life back in America and moved to an obscure hill-station in this country. What prompted this move? They seem to have had other partners, if not spouses, before. Kabir and the tall woman look like they were together and maybe Sujala was dating the young man. Suddenly, I am reminded of the stories Mrs Kashyap had told me about them. About the way the two of them had appeared out of the blue one day. And how a few months later a couple had come looking for them. She had also mentioned that the male visitor had attacked Samir so viciously that he had to be hospitalized; and the way they had subsequently disappeared, leaving poor Samir all alone.

It is possible Samir's downfall started after he was beaten up like that. Violence always leads to more violence. I remember reading somewhere that if you have been violated, you tend to transfer the feeling of aggression on to someone weaker than you.

Is it possible that the young man had attacked Samir because he was possessive about Sujala? But in that case he should have been violent towards Kabir too. Why was Kabir spared and Samir attacked? Where did they all go after that? Why did Sujala come back alone and start living with Samir? There are a million unanswered questions I am confronted with. Besides, I am not even sure whether the young man and the tall woman in the picture are the same individuals who came here a year ago searching for Kabir and Sujala.

There is only one way to find out.

Somehow having an agenda clears my head. I discover I am hungry and go to the kitchen. I make myself toast and eggs after putting the kettle to boil. The thought occurs to me that no matter whom I meet or what friends I make, it's my destiny to be alone. When I was in Coonoor last, I had to stay on my own in Samir's place. Now I am doing the same here.

I wait for nearly an hour after breakfast to venture out. I know Qasim takes a two-hour siesta every afternoon. That is the best time to catch Harini. She is bound to be a lot more comfortable talking to me in his absence. When I come out of the house, Mrs Kashyap's friend is out pottering in her garden. She looks up and gives me an uncertain smile. I nod at her and hurry out of the gate. I get the feeling she wants to talk to me, to ask me something. But I don't have any time to waste.

Harini looks up from behind the counter where she is sitting and reading a Tamil magazine. As usual the store is deserted. No wonder Qasim fleeced all of ten thousand rupees from Kabir's friend when he got the opportunity. I ask her for a moisturizer that I spot on the cosmetics counter. I don't really need it. She comes to Qasim's counter to make a bill. I thrust a five-hundred rupee note at her.

'Don't you have change?' she complains. It is only a hundred and fourteen rupees.'

'It doesn't matter,' I tell her. 'You keep the change. I need some information.'

'What kind of information?' She sounds scared.

I take out the picture in which all of them are posing in Kabir's living room. 'You remember the first time I came to your shop and Kabir had come enquiring about a young man? You said Samir had been earlier to the shop enquiring about the same person.'

She nods, looking confused.

'Was he the same guy you see here?' I thrust the picture at her.

She looks at it and a smile of recognition dawns on her face. 'Yes... he is the same guy. And the woman is also the same.' She starts to look scared again. 'Why do you come here asking all these questions? I spoke to my mother about you. She asked me to stay away from you. She says it's best to avoid any trouble. This job may not pay well but it is steady.'

'I promise I won't tell anyone,' I reassure her.

'But why can't you ask these questions to your friends? You are staying with them, aren't you?'

So everyone in town knows I have been shacking up with Kabir and Sujala. She starts looking for change to hand over to me.

'I told you the change is for you,' I say hastily. 'Please don't mention to anyone that I was here asking questions.'

She nods. 'If Qasim finds out, I am the one he is going to sack.'

'No one is going to tell him,' I reassure her again and turn to leave.

'His name was Nakul,' she says, stopping me in my tracks.

'And what was her name?'

She frowns. 'I can't remember. But I know his name because she kept calling his name and telling him to stop when he was throwing the tables and chairs about. Nakul is one of the Pandavas but that was the first time I came across someone with that name. That is how I remember it.'

I smile at her. I know what my next destination is going to be as soon as I leave the shop.

I knock gently on the door. A dark plump woman in a green nylon sari and a pink sweater opens the door. She must be Harini's cousin who works as a domestic help for Mrs Kashyap. Although she is seeing me for the first time there is a half smile of recognition on her face. It is not just her, the entire town seems to know me. I am the new harlot in town. Strangely it gives me a kind of perverse pleasure to know I am viewed in the same light as Sujala.

'Who is it, Uma?' Mrs Kashyap calls from behind her and then comes into view. She frowns when she sees me.

'May I come in?' I decide to put on my nice schoolgirl act. She isn't fooled this time. She nods curtly and walks back to the sofa on which she has been sitting. She is still knitting for her grandchild. The sweater seems almost ready.

'What do you want?' she asks without looking at me. I am conscious that Uma is still hovering by the door that leads to the inside of the house. 'Should I make some tea?' she asks Mrs Kashyap.

'I don't think Neha is staying that long.'

I find myself going red. She is making it clear to me that I am not wanted. I am the new social outcast who has brought this dubious distinction upon herself.

'I came to enquire whether you were successful in finding a place for me.'

'I thought you had already settled in with those two?' she says with a hint of disapproval in her voice.

'No, that's only temporary. The hotel couldn't accommodate me for more than two days as they had a corporate team coming in for some offsite work. You had already indicated that you weren't interested in taking on a paying guest. They were the only other people I knew in town. I bumped into Sujala the same day, and shared my predicament with her. She said they had to leave for the US soon and needed someone to look after their cottage,' I lie glibly.

'You have been seen taking walks with them just like your friend used to earlier. I saw the three of you one day,' she interjects angrily.

'I did wave out to you but you probably didn't notice that.' This is true. She was the one who had ignored me.

'So you are saying this trip of theirs was pre-planned?' It is evident that her need for gossip is overriding her disapproval.

'Yes. Her sister is getting operated.' This is bizarre. I have no idea I can make up stories so easily. But I really need to have someone on my side; even if it is only old Mrs Kashyap and even though I don't know if she can be of real help.

'She has a sister?' Mrs Kashyap asks dubiously.

'Yes a half sister.'

'What did you want from me?' she asks narrowing her eyes again.

'You mean apart from contacts who can rent me a place?'

She continues to look at me until I lower my gaze.

'If you were really looking for a place to buy, you would have been here much before today,' she says emphatically.

I hesitate. If I admit I have not come looking for her to get help in my house hunting she may get angry with me for telling lies. On the other hand if I continue to insist that I have come to meet her only because I am still looking for a place to move into I won't get the information I am looking for. The canny old woman has got the better of me.

In the end I decide to play safe. 'I came here primarily because with all the contacts you have I thought you would tell me of a place to rent. How long can I go on staying like this with others? But I won't deny the fact that there is also some other information I need.'

She cackles loudly when she hears this. 'Girls today are very smart. We were not as devious in our time.'

I am tempted to tell her I don't see her particularly lacking in that department. But I restrain myself. Instead I get to the point. 'Although I stayed with them for nearly a month, I find them rather strange.'

Mrs Kashyap laughs again. 'You are not the only one who finds them strange.'

'They are very secretive about their past. I have been rather uncomfortable in the past few days,' I complain in a whining voice.

Now I have her attention. She puts aside her knitting and looks at me.

'Strange in what way?' It is clear from her tone that she wants to be titillated. For a moment I toy with the idea of making up stories about Sujala and Kabir practicing black magic. But it may be too much and get me into trouble later on. God alone knows how this strange, disapproving town would react if they heard such things. They would probably put Sujala on a stake and burn her when she gets back.

'Well, sometimes I think he is capable of great violence.' I cannot believe the nonsense I have been churning out to her in the last twenty minutes.

'Does he hit her?' Mrs Kashyap asks interestedly.

'Not in my presence,' I answer reluctantly. I am sure she thinks he does from the way I have responded and my reluctance is because I want to keep it from her.

She looks at me and then looks away. 'It is shameful how some women put up with violence from their husbands. Prashant used to say men who hit women ought to be shot.' Prashant is obviously her deceased husband.

'I agree with him completely,' I tell her not quite meeting her eye. 'That's why I was keen to know whether it was Kabir who beat up Samir last year?' I am no longer surprised at my shameless lies.

'No. From what Mrs Sridhar told me it was the man who had come looking for them. She could hear him screaming and shouting and then she heard the others begging him to stop as he attacked Samir brutally. She almost called the police.' Then she pauses to ask, 'Did they tell you who those visitors were?'

'They told me nothing.'

Realizing this may be the first truth I have told her so far about Sujala and Kabir, she gives me an assessing look. I have unnecessarily complicated matters by coming here. I should have just tapped Mrs Sridhar this morning for all the information I needed. The problem is I don't know her and I can't straight-off launch into asking questions when I meet her.

As if she senses what I am thinking Mrs Kashyap says, 'She thinks you are a snob.'

'Who thinks I am a snob,' I ask, puzzled.

'Mrs Sridhar. She had called me before you came. She said she smiled at you but you ignored her.'

'I am sorry. I was in a hurry at that time,' I tell her. She has just presented me with the opportunity I am looking for. Now I just have to visit Mrs Sridhar and apologize for my behaviour in the morning.

'No one is in a hurry in this town,' Mrs Kashyap says dreamily. 'Not the police. Not the murderer. After killing Karla in that horrific way, he is resting and so are the cops,' she concludes dramatically.

An unexpected visitor

On the way back I decide to drop in at Mrs Sridhar's house. She was the one who had heard all the shouting and seen an injured Samir being carted to the hospital that day. She could have seen something that might shed light on the identity of the man who attacked Samir. However when I ring her bell a woman who resembles the help at Mrs Kashyap's house opens the door. I tell her I want to speak to the lady of the house. She asks me to wait and goes inside, re-emerging after a few minutes. 'Madam says she will let you know when you can meet her.'

I stand there and gape. This is something totally unexpected. I have not been turned away like this from anyone's door before. And then I remember the way Mrs Sridhar had looked up at me from her gardening with a smile this morning and how curtly I had ignored her. This was her revenge. I go back to the cottage cursing myself for not having spared a few minutes in the morning to make small talk with her.

I let myself in and go directly to the kitchen to get myself a glass of water, and freeze. There is someone in the room upstairs. Are they back? But I cannot hear any conversation, just the sound of someone moving around. My heart beating wildly I edge towards the stairway and stand listening. There is silence, as if the person upstairs has also sensed that I am in the cottage. The door creaks open and I can see a pair of long legs in a pair of jeans coming down the stairs.

'It's you! What are you doing here?' I scream at him. Samir seems to have lost tonnes of weight since I last saw him. He looks gaunt, all the more so because his hair is cropped short and he is limping a bit. His good looks seem to have faded a bit. I stand there and gawk foolishly at him. Comprehension dawns in his eyes slowly.

'Have you been living here?' he asks coldly.

All I can do is to nod.

'You can't be serious. What's wrong with you?' he accuses, coming close to me. There is a dangerous glint in his eyes.

I suddenly find my voice. 'I should be asking what you are doing in someone else's house. How did you let yourself in?'

Multiple expressions flit across his face. Samir has always been transparent that way. You can read his intent in his eyes; he is trying to figure out how much he should tell me.

'I came to look for my painting,' he admits finally. I continue to stare blankly at him. What's he talking about?

'I came back to my cottage this morning and found the nude missing. I thought it most likely that she took it in my absence and came here to confront her. But when I rang the bell, no one opened the door and so I let myself in to search for it,' he explains.

'You have a spare key to this place?'

'No, not really!' he says awkwardly.

'How did you open the door then?'

'I discovered a long time ago that our doors have similar locks and the key to my cottage can open hers as well,' he confesses slyly. 'She doesn't know about it.'

'That's disgusting. How could you?' I find myself getting angry at Samir on Sujala's behalf.

'What are you getting so antsy about?'

'What's wrong with you? Even if she has it, it's her painting. She has more of a right over it.'

He advances towards me and twists my arm. 'Where has she hidden it?'

'Let go of me,' I scream. 'You are hurting me.' I push him away with all my strength and he almost falls. Jolted to reality, Samir stands looking at me, shock and disbelief writ large on his face.

'Go away! Get out of this house. Otherwise I am going outside and shouting for help!' I scream.

He sits down on one of the steps, his head in his hands. My anger spent, my arm smarting from the bruises he has left on it, I watch him warily. My childhood friend has turned into a monstrous enemy. When did we let this happen to us?

He raises his head and looks searchingly at me.

'Come back with me,' he pleads.

'No,' I say emphatically. 'I am not going anywhere with you.'

'Why? Has she been poisoning your mind against me?'

'I am not interested in discussing her with you.'

'You sound as if you are in love with her.'

'You make it sound like a crime. Considering you were stalking her not so long ago I find your disapproval funny.'

'So it's true,' he sounds more shocked than angry. 'Jesus, Neha. What do you know about her?'

Once again I have no answers. Whenever I am in Samir's presence I find it difficult to believe he had anything to do with Mother's murder. I am confiding things to him as if nothing has happened and we are back to being school chums.

'I know as much about her as you do,' I claim bravely.

'I doubt it,' he says with a snigger.

I am not sure what to say. Here is my chance to ask him all the questions I have been living with for all these days. About Mother, about Kabir and Sujala, about the couple who visited them last year and the man who attacked Samir. I have been running around in circles since morning to find out all this and the one person who can give me all the answers is sitting in front of me. But the tension and hostility we have generated in the last few minutes makes civilized conversation impossible. Not to mention Mother's death that's always going to come between us until the murderer is found. For a long time all we can do is stare at each other in silence. He is the first to cave in.

'I don't blame you,' he says. 'I have experienced what you are going through. When she casts a spell, it's impossible to come out of it. I hope you know, none of the others can ever be important to her. It's him she cares about. She will do anything to keep him with her.'

Vijay Nair

How do I know he is speaking about Kabir and her? Plain intuition, I guess, or maybe a shared insight two persons have when one is living with the same thing the other has undergone earlier. I can't hold back any more. 'Who were the two who came looking for them last year? Was the man her earlier husband or was it the woman who used to be married to him when they were in the US?'

He throws back his head and laughs.

'What's the matter?'

'From what the two of you seem to share, you can do better than that at the guessing game.'

'Maybe you can make a start by not playing these games with me,' I snap.

He gets up slowly from the stairs and walks towards me. Bringing his face really close to mine, he almost whispers in my ears: 'They were their partners. It was one happy family when they were together in the US.' I am startled by Samir's bitter laugh after he has confirmed my worst fears.

I draw in my breath. 'You mean to say the woman was Kabir's partner and the man hers?

He starts to laugh again. 'No, the man was Kabir's partner and the woman was hers when they were all living in Lincoln, Nebraska.'

I think he has gone mad. I can't make any sense of what he is saying. 'You don't believe me, do you? But that's the truth. Kabir and Nakul were lovers and so were Chetna and Sujala. From what I have been told, Kabir and Chetna were teaching in the same university and they were also great friends. Nakul is a graduate student in the same university. He is from Chandigarh. I think Kabir also went to the US

159

as a graduate student many years ago and after getting his PhD started teaching there.'

I am sure he is making all this up. He will laugh some more at my incredulous expression and mock me. Instead he continues earnestly, 'To cut a long story short, Nakul's folks were getting a little suspicious about their son and were desperate to see him married. There was relentless pressure on him. His mother is a heart patient or maybe she pretended to be sick. You know these Punjabi families.'

'I don't follow anything you are saying.'

'Wait… give me time to complete the story,' he says dragging me by my hand to the living room where he flops on one of the chairs.

Samir tells me Kabir was very protective towards Nakul. The young man used to have these attacks of rage from time to time. The shrinks had diagnosed it as bipolar disorder and prescribed medication that Nakul refused to take. He felt they made him put on weight.

Kabir had taken him to an ayurvedic practitioner but his medicines hadn't proved to be very effective either. Whenever another letter full of recriminations and emotional blackmail arrived from his mother, Nakul would get all stressed out. He would rave and rant and throw things around the house. There were times he got self-destructive, giving in to violent bouts of rage. Once he was arrested for smashing his classmate's car for some silly fight they had over a poker game. Since these spells corresponded with letters or phone calls from his parents, Kabir decided the best way to stop these provocations was for Nakul to have a marriage of convenience that would stop his mother from emotionally blackmailing him.

Kabir was aware many same sex couples from the subcontinent living in the US entered into an arrangement with other same sex couples of the opposite gender and got married to each other to please families back home. He managed to convince Chetna that Nakul and Sujala should get married. And then Chetna came up with the madcap idea that Kabir and she should also marry at the same time. That way all of them could experience an Indian wedding and go for a honeymoon together.

That was the plan, and they were all excited about it like schoolchildren plotting a prank. It was Sujala who suggested another variation to the devious plan. She convinced the others that it might be better if she married Kabir as he was the older guy and Nakul married Chetna – the older woman. She felt everyone who came for the weddings would think of it as true love then. 'She said she meant it as a joke, but from what I have learnt about her devious ways, she may have wanted Kabir for herself all along,' Samir concludes with a bitter laugh.

Apparently, complications arose soon after the wedding:

'Since Kabir's folks were in Delhi, and Nakul's in Chandigarh, the weddings were held in two different cities on the same day. Rajasthan had been picked as their common honeymoon destination. While Kabir and Sujala were ready to leave for their honeymoon a day after they were married, Nakul's more conservative parents wanted Chetna and him to visit their ancestral home in the village after the ceremony was over. They were asked to go for their honeymoon three days after the wedding. As it turned out, the excitement of the wedding was too much for Nakul's mother and she fell ill on the day they were meant to leave. Nakul and Chetna had to stay back in Chandigarh for a few days more until she recovered. There was no way Kabir and Sujala could have returned without raising the suspicions of both the families. Also, Samir said, he wasn't sure whether anyone from Sujala or Chetna's family had come down for the nuptials. He hadn't asked and Sujala hadn't volunteered any information. But if they had, maybe there were more than two sets of families who needed to be convinced about the reasons for Kabir and Sujala sacrificing their honeymoon. The four were separated – much to Chetna's consternation, as she was the one who had to play the dutiful daughter-in-law.'

According to Samir, Kabir and Sujala hung around in Rajasthan, travelling and sightseeing, and she used the time to ensnare Kabir.

'It's a bit funny, but by the time Nakul and Chetna reached Rajasthan, these two had eloped. It was funny in that they were married to each other and had to elope to escape from their lovers! They left word at the hotel that they had to rush back to the US due to an emergency. Puzzled by this, Nakul and Chetna decided to follow suit. The original plan was that after a fortnight's holiday all four would go to Kabir's house in Delhi for a week and leave from there. Now all their plans had gone awry. Kabir and Sujala had disappeared and were incommunicado for all practical purposes. Nakul and Chetna went back to Lincoln only to find their partners weren't there either. Kabir had taken a sabbatical and the university couldn't tell them where he was and when he would return. Sujala's parents were equally clueless about her. As it is, her traditional father had disowned her as soon as he had found out she was living with another woman. The stepmother had never been able to connect to the strange girl anyway. They felt her half-sister knew something but she gave nothing away. When Chetna called Kabir's family in Delhi, they professed ignorance about his whereabouts but didn't seem unduly worried, making her suspect they knew where he was but had been told by them to keep it a secret.'

'Why couldn't they just tell Nakul and Chetna that they were in love with each other?' I ask as if I am talking about two characters I have come across in a story.

'I have no idea. I think Kabir has always been a bit scared of Nakul. There is no telling what he might do when he is in one of his rages.'

'What about Chetna?' I persist. This is such a bizarre tale. I still don't know whether to believe it.

'I don't think it is hard for Sujala to use and discard others,' Samir spits out angrily. 'Now she is using you just like she used me.'

'Using me for *what*?' I ask, bewildered.

'To keep him with her.'

'What do you mean?'

'Well, I think Kabir is really torn between her and Nakul. At least when I was hanging around with them, he was going through a lot of guilt over what he had done to Nakul. I guess I provided the right kind of distraction for him. She must have felt that if she managed to get Kabir interested in me, he was not likely to dump her for Nakul.'

'You are going too fast for me. Please explain everything properly,' I implore.

So Samir began from the beginning:

Samir first met Sujala and Kabir one afternoon when they were walking in the hills. He had driven down to his favourite spot with his easel and was painting a landscape when they appeared out of nowhere. They had stopped to marvel at his work. In a town full of old pensioners Samir had found their company refreshing. They had invited him home for lunch and the three of them had bonded over Samir's fascinating account of his experiences in Paris; Sujala had never been to France and had an insatiable curiosity about the place.

After that they had started meeting often and Samir had found himself falling in love with her. 'Maybe I was already smitten when I saw her in the hills that first time. She was in a yellow shirt, she's always been partial to that colour and I thought I had never seen a woman so luminously beautiful.'

I know what he means. I have felt like that about her, especially in the afternoons when I walked beside her. He may as well be telling my story.

Apparently, Kabir suggested that Samir paint his wife's portrait. She seemed unreasonably happy with the proposal. At first Samir was naïve enough to believe she was ecstatic because he was painting her and that she too was fighting an attraction towards him.

'I figured out much later it was because he had wanted her to be painted. To her it was proof that she meant a great deal to Kabir.' But none of this mattered while he was painting her. For Samir it was enough that he could spend long hours painting her.

He spent many evenings with them after the painting sessions were over, smoking weed and staying on for dinner. He was aware about all the gossip surrounding the three of them but he didn't care. One evening, when the portrait was almost done, Kabir suggested that he paint Sujala in the nude. Sujala had giggled and snuggled up to her husband while Samir couldn't believe his ears. His only apprehension was about how he would restrain himself when she took her clothes off in his presence.

But before any of that happened, Chetna and Nakul had turned up in town. Worried to death after months of waiting for their lovers, they had come back to India and employed a private detective. The sleuth had followed the tracks of the missing duo to the hotel in Coonoor. They had checked into the same hotel and made their enquiries. One of the waiters told them that Kabir and Sujala had decided to stay on in Coonoor but he didn't know where. He had vaguely mentioned Upper Coonoor. So they had spent an entire morning going from place to place in search of their ex-lovers. They had managed to locate them only when they went to the departmental store and Harini told them where they lived.

Samir was in the cottage when they knocked on the door. All three of them were pleasantly high when the visitors barged in. Kabir had asked Samir to stay for dinner and he was looking forward to eating with the two of them. 'I had overindulged that day. I had rolled a couple of joints at home before starting out to paint Sujala. And then I smoked some more with them. I was high as a kite and felt the world loved me and I loved the world. Things couldn't have been more beautiful. So when the visitors forced their way in with an uncontrollable Nakul screaming and shouting, I was a little taken aback. Sujala coaxed Chetna and Nakul to hold off the discussion until all of us had dinner. Kabir was baking that day; he excused himself and went into the kitchen to make more food than he had originally planned. Sujala went upstairs with Chetna to their bedroom while Nakul paced the living room agitatedly. I followed Kabir to the kitchen to check whether he needed help. I have no idea when that bastard sneaked up from behind and attacked me.'

'Why did he attack you?'

'Search me. I told you he is a psycho and you can't expect psychos to back their actions with reason. He must have been crazy enough to believe that Kabir and I were having a scene. He crept up behind me and brought a saucepan down on my head; I nearly passed out. Then he started to kick me, cursing and shouting while I looked at Kabir for help.'

'What did he do?'

'He was trying to pull Nakul away from me when Nakul turned and punched him in his face and stomach. The guy fights really dirty. I could see from where I lay on the floor that Kabir's nose was bleeding. Then he pushed Kabir against the kitchen counter and pulled down his trousers. He fucked him right there and then, cursing all the time.'

'I am sure you are making up all this,' I say disbelievingly. 'Where were Chetna and Sujala when all this was happening?'

'God knows. Maybe the two dykes were balling each other when their men were screwing downstairs.'

I am appalled by Samir's choice of words and aghast at what he has told me about the night he was attacked. The whole thing sounds unreal; as if Samir has made up another story. And yet it seems to fit in with Kabir and Sujala's strange behaviour.

Kabir and Chetna took Samir to the hospital. He had fractured his arm and had suffered a mild concussion. Kabir pleaded with Samir to tell the hospital authorities that it was an accident; to say he had tripped and a heavy vase had come crashing down on him. Samir did as he was told. Sujala visited him the next day. She promised to tell him everything the next time she visited the hospital. She claimed to be in a hurry as she had to go back and help Kabir with the cooking. Later in the evening Kabir came down with Nakul and made him apologize to Samir. After what he had witnessed in the kitchen the previous day, Samir had been too embarrassed to talk to the two men.

Sujala didn't visit him after that. Neither she nor Kabir dropped in for the duration of his hospital stay. Samir kept on making excuses for her. Vrinda had landed up a couple of days after hearing about her son and he made himself believe they were afraid of encountering his mother. When he was discharged, he asked Vrinda's driver to drive him to their cottage first. It was locked.

'I went crazy after that. They simply vanished from my life; I felt my world had crumbled.'

I can understand what he must have gone through; I almost went to pieces myself when they left.

'I didn't know anyone who knew them. I had heard her mention that Kabir's folks were in Delhi– '

'Yeah, you mentioned they were married in Delhi,' I interject, eager to know what happened next.

Samir continues: 'I called up the university in Nebraska. I wasn't surprised at the response they gave me. They said Kabir was on a sabbatical but they didn't know where he was. That's when I called up Ratna. I was desperate to find Sujala and I thought that your father, with all his contacts in Delhi, would be able to find out about Kabir's family and that would lead me to her.'

'What did my mother say?'

'She told me to come to Lucknow and said she would have a meeting arranged between your father and me.'

'Did she charge you for it?'

'Charge me? Charge me for what?'

'Did you have to pay her a commission?'

'What are you talking about? Are you nuts? Why would she charge me for getting to meet your dad?'

'Your mother said she was willing to pay a commission to Ma to organize a meeting with my father.'

'That must have been business. This was personal,' he sounds angry that I can harbour such uncharitable thoughts about my mother.

'So you knew she did all this wheeling-dealing using my father?'

'Yes... of course. That's how the cookie crumbles in the world of business. Why do you think I want to have nothing to do with it?'

The whole world knew my mother was into shady

transactions except me. And they say children keep things from their parents.

'But then when I went to her flat... I noticed the door was ajar. I thought your maid must have stepped out for something, leaving it open. I knocked but no one came to the door. So I went in. It was around six thirty in the evening and dusk was falling. She was sprawled out on the living room floor. It was horrible. There was so much blood. I just stood there looking at her. I was petrified. Whoever had done it, had bashed her face in and one of her eyes had almost fallen out. I couldn't move for a few minutes. And then the telephone rang. I just ran out of the place and went back to the hotel where I was staying. I thought to call you but I wasn't thinking straight that evening. I was afraid I would be arrested and then I would never be able to find Sujala. That's how obsessed I was with her in those days. I didn't care for anything or anyone else. I am sorry about lying to you when you called afterwards from Lucknow,' he says shamefacedly.

According to Samir, he had lost it completely after that. He stopped painting. He sat in front of the computer everyday Googling their names. He thought of employing a private sleuth to track them down like Nakul and Chetna had. He even approached a couple but they told him the information he had about them was too inadequate for them to get anywhere with their search.

Just as suddenly as she had vanished, she reappeared on his doorstep after a few months. When he'd opened the door, she had rushed straight into his arms and they had made love on the living room floor. Initially he was

so happy to have her back that it hadn't occurred to him
to ask her where Kabir was. They tried to maintain their
separate cottages but it didn't work. She didn't know anyone
apart from him in town. Everything in her cottage reminded
her of Kabir, so she moved in with Samir. That's when
he started painting her in the nude. She spent her days
brooding but he was too happy to give it much importance.
He felt everything would turn out fine now that she was
back. Vrinda heard about the woman who was living with
her son and dropped by to check her out. She disapproved
of Sujala from the moment they met.

'Mum has always been a pain. But this time she was
right,' Samir says ruefully.

Sujala would often cry in her sleep and call out Kabir's
name. She was depressed. Bit by bit, Samir had been able
to prise out the entire story from her. Her past didn't matter
to him. What was important was that she was with him, and
he felt there could be nothing more precious than that. He
thought if she had something to occupy her, she might come
out of her depression. So he spoke to Karla. As it turned
out, one of the junior-school teachers had suddenly gone
on leave to care for her husband who had suffered a stroke
and there was a temporary vacancy. Sujala had never taught
before but was willing to give it a try. More importantly,
Karla was enthusiastic about having her on board although
she knew that Sujala had no training as a teacher and had
dropped out of college after her sophomore year.

'I guess I was so much in love with her that I didn't
think of the possibility that dykes can recognize each other,'
Samir says bitterly. I bristle when I hear him say this but

at the same time I don't want to shout at him lest he clams up on me.

After a few weeks of joining school, Samir noticed that Sujala was becoming increasingly aloof. She refused to let him touch her. Every Sunday afternoon she would disappear saying she wanted to go for a walk on her own. Initially he was indulgent but then he began to get angry at her indifference. He followed her one day and was shocked to see her go to Karla's house, which was located behind the school.

'Something made me go to the back of the house. I noticed a glass window that opened to the side of the cottage. It was shut with the curtains drawn but there was a chink through which I could peer inside the bedroom.

'They were at it, tearing each other's clothes off. I was furious. I went and banged on the door till Karla was forced to open it. I dragged Sujala back to the cottage with me.'

Samir can be such a child. Did he really think he could end an affair like that?

Things went steadily downhill after that. Samir forbade Sujala from working in the school. She refused. When things got ugly, she went back to her cottage even though he needed her to sit for the painting. He went back to her, begging and pleading to be given a second chance but she refused to move back with him. She started spending more and more time at Karla's. Samir barged in a couple of times threatening Karla with exposure. He was that desperate. Karla called up Vrinda and complained to her.

'It was all quite embarrassing. You know Mum. She came rushing here to tell me I should be happy Sujala is out of my life.'

A couple of months later, Kabir reappeared in Coonoor just as suddenly as she had. Samir found out that Sujala had stopped going to school after that. She also broke off all ties with Karla who didn't seem to be distraught at the betrayal. The two women seemed to have called it quits without much heartburn.

Samir made a couple of unsuccessful attempts to get back on the same footing with the couple. But they were determined not to have anything to do with him.

'I fucked up big time. I lost all semblance of dignity and started stalking her. Whenever we met, she would shoo me off like I was a rabid dog. The more she insulted me, the more desperate I got. I don't know why they didn't file a police complaint against me.' Samir is visibly calmer now. As if sharing everything with me has lightened the burden he has been carrying all this while.

'How did you recover from all this mess?' I ask him.

He shakes his head. 'It's so strange. Mum took me to Coimbatore for a few days. Until I went back home I used to wake up calling out her name in my sleep. But as soon as I was back in my room, I was free of her. I went back to my painting and the next time I thought of her was when I found myself next to Karla's corpse in her house – which had been subjected to the exact same brutal treatment as Ratna's body,' he chokes as if overcome by the memory.

'What were you doing in her cottage?'

'I found a note from Karla under my door one morning asking me to come and meet her urgently. I called her number but no one responded. It was a Sunday and the school was closed. So I decided to go and meet her. I had always felt a little guilty about the way I had abused her

when I had discovered Sujala and she were balling each
other and felt meeting her would give me the opportunity
to apologize and make amends. With Sujala out of the
equation, I didn't hold anything against her. Both of us had
lost out to Kabir. Besides Aunty Karla was very sweet to me
when I was a kid. She always remembered my birthdays.'

'She had signed this note?' I ask.

'No. It was typewritten and so I should have smelt a rat.
But at that time, I didn't think of it. I drove down to her
place, leaving the note behind at the cottage. I couldn't
find it afterwards.'

His phone rings just then. He takes the call and listens
intently. 'Okay. I will meet you soon,' he says before
hanging up.

'Who was it?' I ask.

'Randeep,' he says getting up. 'You won't believe how
supportive he has been. And do you know I had a really
bitter fight with him before I left for Lucknow to meet your
mother? He had come over to my cottage to tell me that all
the mess I was creating in my personal life was impacting
Mum's health. I let him have it. I told him I couldn't help
it if I was more important to my mother than he was. And
with all that was going on in my life, I didn't have the
time to have a pointless discussion with him. Later I felt
bad about how I had spoken to him and told him I would
meet him after I returned from Lucknow. But so many
things happened after that. It took me a long time to get
over Ratna's death and then Sujala came back and I forgot
everything else. I just kept ignoring him. I made up with
him only after I got arrested. I misunderstood him all along.
He has done so much to keep me out of trouble.'

I am hardly listening to him. I am yet to recover from everything he's shared with me about Sujala. I suddenly realize Samir has got up and is leaving the cottage. 'Wait,' I call out to him.

Samir groans. 'Why do you always call out to me when I am leaving? That's one evil omen I believe in. Don't you think I have had enough bad luck to last me a lifetime?'

'If you are truly over her, why are you going to such lengths to get the nude back?' I ask, ignoring his remark.

'Call it an artist's vanity. It's one of my best paintings. Likely to endure,' he winks at me as he gets up to leave. 'I will come by tomorrow to fetch you. Please pack your stuff and be ready to move out. I would have taken you with me tonight itself, but Mum and Randeep Uncle are coming over tonight with some dinner. Maybe it's best if Mum doesn't know you are here,' he tells me. I can hear him whistling softly as he goes out of the house.

It's only when I hear his car pull out of the driveway that I realize I have forgotten to ask him where he has been all these days. Was he in the hospital or was he in some secret hide-away till Vrinda used her contacts to extricate him from this legal tangle?

Waxy mask of death

I wait for Samir in the morning although I have no plans of going back with him to his cottage. If everything he has told me about them is true, I stand a much better chance with Sujala. She and Chetna were lovers before she got married to Kabir. She left Samir to be with Karla. Her preference is obvious. Maybe Kabir became important to her because she couldn't find the right woman. Maybe by this time she has started tiring of him. Why else did she want me to stay with them? I am sure she wants to test me for a while because she does not want to be let down by yet another woman. I will do everything to live up to her expectations. She has suffered a lot and I am going to spend the rest of my life taking care of her.

I switch on the music system and put on a Begum Akhtar CD from Kabir's collection of ghazals. When the melodious voice wafts through the room singing *Kabhi hum me tum me karar tha, tumhe yaad ho ke na yaad ho,* I close my eyes and imagine the two of us holding each other. Kabir can stay. I don't mind him as long as he doesn't come between us. I am going to give the relationship everything I have. The reverie is broken by a knock at the door. I get up thinking it must be Samir. I am surprised to find Mrs Sridhar's help standing outside. She thrusts a note in my hand – 'Madam asked me to give this to you,' she says shyly and disappears. I read the note standing on the threshold.

> *Dear Neha,*
>
> *I am pleased to invite you for high tea, today at 5 p.m. I have also requested Pinky to join us. I believe the two of you met while you were staying at Samir's cottage. You may dress informally if you want, but no scruffy jeans please.*
>
> *Fond regards,*
> *Dolly*

I try hard to contain the laughter bubbling up inside me. The old crone is totally batty. She writes as if she is the queen of England. And I can't get over the fact her name is Dolly and her friend is called Pinky. Things are getting really surreal in this place. But I know I have to accept the invitation. If only to ferret out any more information they can give me about Kabir and Sujala.

But once I get back to the room, I can't bear the music anymore and switch it off. There is something unhealthy about all this. I came back to Coonoor with a purpose. To find out who murdered my mother. Instead I seem to have got seduced into something else altogether. I am no longer thinking about Mother's brutal death. Sujala has become much more important to me. And the irony is I don't even know whether I matter to her. Neither of them has bothered to stay in touch after they left.

I feel alone and helpless sitting there. I cannot leave the cottage they have entrusted in my care. Once they return, I can focus my energies on finding out who killed my mother. After listening to Samir yesterday, I am convinced he has nothing to do with it. I am sure he was telling the truth when he said he discovered that Mother had been killed when he went to meet her.

Once Sujala is back everything will be easier. Her physical presence alone will soothe the turmoil I feel inside me and clear my head. All I have to do is wait.

I decide to disregard the bit in the note about dressing informally and deck myself up. I choose a magenta dress from the collection Mother had put together for me. I match it with heavy silver jewellery and carefully make up my face. I feel like a courtesan from the last century but the stranger that I spy in the mirror looks like an attractive woman, aware of the sensuality she exudes. I am hoping Samir is not going to turn up just when I am leaving and spoil everything by laughing at me.

This time it's Mrs Sridhar who opens the door and stands critically appraising me. She nods at me and gestures to me to follow her inside. For someone who wanted her guests to come informally dressed to her party, she has not spared any effort. Her thinning hair is freshly shampooed and blow dried and there is a dash of rouge on her cheeks. Her lips are coloured pink and her eyes flecked with green shadow to match the pale green jump suit she is wearing with an emerald-coloured stole. Her face looks older than Mrs Kashyap's and her strange ensemble and loud make-up highlight her wrinkles rather than conceal them. She looks like a witch without her broomstick.

'I was the first runner-up in the Miss India contest in the sixties,' she says settling down in a comfortable chair.

I am taken aback by her opening statement and don't know how to react. Not that it matters. She is not paying much attention to me anyway, having decided to go back into the past. 'Those days, the pageants weren't what they are now. I stitched my own gown for the finals. All I got after coming so close to winning was a hamper full of cosmetics. The girls today make millions but we were content with seeing our pictures in the newspaper. We were absolute naturals. Not like these cosmetic marvels you have today,' she pauses and narrows her eyes at me. 'Do you know, they all have nose jobs,' she announces in a shrill voice.

'Who has nose jobs?' I ask. I am no longer sure it was such a great idea to accept her invitation.

'All the Miss Indias we have had in the past decade. Even Aishwarya. I know her aunt. She told me.'

I smile nervously at her.

'Kamla,' she bellows loudly. Her help appears immediately as if she was listening outside the door.

'Is everything ready?'

'Yes, Amma.'

'Okay. We will have our tea as soon as Pinky arrives,' she says dismissing Kamla with a regal wave and turning to me again. This time she makes me jump with her question. 'Why are you staying with those spies?'

'I beg your pardon?'

'Don't act innocent with me. I am sure you know the couple you are staying with are CIA agents.'

'I don't think so,' I protest lamely. 'They are just different.'

She snorts and looks away. 'In that case, why do they keep coming and going? Even if they are not spies, I am sure they are mixed up in some shady business. Drug peddling, perhaps,' she speculates aloud. I realize she is not looking for a conversation. She just wants me to be an audience to her performance. She leans back and closes her eyes. I have no idea what I am supposed to do.

'I was offered a role in the film *Jewel Thief*. Opposite Dev Anand. He was so handsome those days. But my father wouldn't hear of it. He felt I had disgraced the family enough by wearing a swimsuit for the Miss India pageant. All his relatives had stopped talking to him. So he decided to get me married to Vishnu. He proved to be a good husband. He was very good in bed,' she says and smiles slyly. I am too embarrassed to respond.

She stares blankly ahead and then blushes suddenly as if the virile Vishnu is present in the room waiting to make love to her. The silence gets too much for me so I give a polite cough. That breaks her trance. When she turns to speak to me, her eyes are full of mischief. 'Are you a virgin?' she asks loudly.

I have had enough. I am not going to take any more nonsense from her. 'No,' I say boldly. 'I stopped being one at fourteen.'

'That's a good age to lose your cherry,' she exclaims and breaks into peals of laughter. Thankfully the telephone rings just then and Kamala comes running into the room to take the call. She mutters a hello and then listens carefully to what is being said. She breaks into a volley of Tamil exclamations and then hangs up. She turns towards us, trembling, and says, 'Pinky Amma is dead. Uma came to work and found the door open. When she went in she found Amma on the floor. She says there is blood everywhere.' She starts to cry.

We have to call for a taxi. Mrs Sridhar suffers from arthritis and can't walk all the way. She has been crying ever since we have heard the news. The tears have smudged her make-up and there are streaks of green and black on her face. She looks like a clown rather than a former beauty queen, with an air of overwhelming sadness about her.

A small crowd stands in front of Mrs Kashyap's house. Two policemen ensure no one gets in past the gate. They look at us impatiently when our taxi stops and we start walking up the drive.

'Madam, you can't go in,' one of them says.

'I was like family to her,' Mrs Sridhar protests and before he can say anything, pushes him out of her way and sails inside the gate. Once inside, she turns and looks at me. 'She is also with me. A friend of the family,' she announces sternly. They dare not stop me after she has been so overbearing with them.

Inside, are two police officers who turn to look at us. One of them is familiar. I realize he is the same man who was in the police station when I had gone there with Vrinda after Samir's accident. He smiles at us uncertainly. The man with him is a forensic specialist who has been called in to determine the cause and time of death. He looks at us impatiently and then turning to the station in-charge shrugs his shoulders.

Mrs Kashyap's body is on the ground, covered with a white sheet. Mrs Sridhar walks towards it. She is shivering.

'Madam, stay away from the body! Who allowed you to come inside?' protests the man from the police station. Undeterred, Mrs Sridhar walks up to the corpse and flings the cover aside. I am not sure whether the scream I hear echoing around the room emanates from me or her.

So this is what she must have looked like. Mrs Kashyap's face looks like a hideous mask. It has been battered beyond recognition. One eye bulges out and the half of her face visible from where I stand is a bloody mess. Her hands are tied together and lie limply on her chest. There are streaks of blood in her snowy hair. Mrs Sridhar is on her knees moaning gently. I am ready to throw up then and there. I run outside to get some fresh air while the doctor rushes to be at Mrs Sridhar's side.

The man from the station comes out of the house and goes towards the gate. He is gesturing furiously to the policemen stationed outside for letting the two of us come in. I walk towards the fence that separates Mrs Kashyap's cottage from Samir's.

Where has he disappeared?

Mrs Sridhar informs me later that the policemen told her that Mrs Kashyap was killed earlier in the afternoon. They estimate the time of death between two and four p.m. Samir may have been in his cottage when Mrs Kashyap was being murdered. Unless, of course, he committed the crime. I push the thought away from my head. Samir can't be the murderer. The friend I know is too intelligent to kill his neighbour when he is already the prime suspect in a similar murder case. The murderer has to be someone who hates Samir enough to want to put him behind bars for life and will not stop at anything to achieve his goals.

I decide to go for a walk again to clear my head. I am tense and anxious, not to mention grief-stricken. I didn't know Mrs Kashyap well enough to think of her as a friend. What I do know is that she didn't deserve a death bereft of dignity. No one deserves a death like that. None of them, not Mother, not Karla and not this old lady with twinkling eyes who had wanted to protect me from Sujala.

I shudder. It could be my turn next. I wonder who will mourn me if that happens.

I am not sure why but somewhere along the way I get the feeling I am being followed. I turn back twice or thrice but see no one. A lone cyclist passes me from the opposite side; he is too weighed down by the cold to notice me. A woman with a small child comes from behind. She is carrying some dried sticks on her head. The child turns her snot-covered face towards me to smile at me uncertainly. I feel a sudden lump in my throat. They may be poor and suffering but at least they are together.

I want to go to Samir's cottage to check whether he is there. But I know it's foolish to do so with the place teeming with police. I wonder if he is hiding in his studio. I had noticed the gate was locked from outside when I entered Mrs Kashyap's house. But there is also a back gate to the cottage through which he could have slipped in. I dismiss the thought. He is a suspect in Karla's murder. The cops are sure to search the house, locked gate or not. I don't think they need anyone's permission to do so.

I am a real freak of nature. All that has happened since evening should have killed my appetite, but I feel ravenous. After many days of abstinence I feel like eating a full meal. I go into the kitchen and make myself some steaming khichdi with lots of vegetables thrown in. It used to be Mother's comfort food. She used to say no matter how bleak her mood was, if she had the khichdi made by Jamuna, it made her feel she could take on anyone.

I eat too much and start to feel drowsy immediately afterwards. I go to my room and fall asleep.

I am walking down a road lined with trees and there are tears streaming down my face. I am not sure what I am crying about except that it feels very cold and I seem to be somewhere away from civilization, utterly lost. Suddenly a cold arm snakes out from behind a tree. I am speechless with shock.

'Neha, wake up. It's me, Samir.' He manages to sound tense and upset at the same time.

'What… who is it?' I sit up shivering and switch on the bedside lamp. 'Samir? What are you doing here?'

'I didn't know where else to go,' he says miserably. I have been on the run ever since I saw Mrs Kashyap's dead body. Why is this happening to me?'

'When did you see her?' I ask.

'I can't remember. Maybe late in the afternoon. Last night Mum had brought back some food from Coimbatore for me. Stuff like bread, eggs, cheese, ham etc. She told me to speak to Mrs Kashyap about a new maid for me in the morning. I woke up late and kept putting it off. I made myself some sandwiches and spent some time cleaning up the house a bit. And then I started to read a book. That's when I was startled by a scream from Mrs Kashyap's house.

At first I thought I was imagining it. You know I have been having these nightmares since last year. But I kept on feeling uneasy. So I decided to go and check on her,' he pauses, searching for words. 'It was horrible to see her like that. Her corpse looked just like your mother's did when she had been murdered, and then Karla and now this poor old lady,' his voice is choked, he is overcome with emotion.

'What did you do when you saw the body? I hope you didn't call anyone,' I ask, my voice unsteady.

'Are you mad? Not after what happened with Karla,' he snaps and then continues, 'You know I have a feeling the murderer was in the house all the time. There was just a fifteen minute gap between the time I heard the scream and I went inside to investigate. And while I was contemplating whether I should go to her place, I had gone to the living room and was looking out of the window. Nobody came out of the house.'

'Oh... Samir. Why didn't you go inside the house and search for whoever was hiding?'

'Because my first impulse was to run away as far from the scene of crime as possible,' he says brokenly. 'You have no idea how terrible the two nights I spent in the lock-up the last time were. There were rats in that cell and you know how frightened I am of them.'

Maybe it is the tension. But I start laughing when he says that.

'What's so funny?' Samir admonishes.

I continue to giggle in spite of myself. 'You are too much. Talking about your fear of rats when you have so many other things to worry about.'

He stares blankly at me and then joins in the giggling. 'You are such a bitch. It's a matter of life and death for me and you are laughing at me...'

'I can't help it. How can you be such an ass and always land up at the scene of the crime?'

'I don't know,' he says ruefully and starts to laugh too. It is contagious. We are unable to stop, spurring each other's laughter, until a new thought strikes me. 'Where have you been since the time you discovered the body?' I ask.

'Hiding,' he says turning miserable again. 'There is a place in the hills where I go to paint in the afternoon. I was there until it got too cold.'

'I hope you didn't call anybody.'

'Are you nuts? However influential Ma is, if they find out I was at the scene of the crime again, nothing and nobody can save me. The only person I can trust is you. In fact I followed you for a little while this evening and then realized if we were seen talking to each other in a public place, you could also get into trouble.'

'Oh Samir...' I say again quite overcome with emotions. On an impulse I hug him tightly. 'Have you had anything to eat?'

'No, I am famished. Is there anything to eat?'

'I'll rustle up some toast and eggs for you, and maybe some coffee?' I am fussing over him like he is a small child.

'That would be lovely,' he says, getting into my bed and drawing my quilt around his neck.

When I come back with the food and the coffee, he is fast asleep, snoring gently. I leave the tray on the bedside table. He can heat the food and coffee when he wakes up. I make my way to the room upstairs. In a perverse sort of a way I am happy that Samir has taken my bed. It gives me an opportunity to sleep on hers. I lie on it, thinking about what she would be doing at that moment. It must be daytime wherever she is. Are they together? The thought is unbearable. Instead I go back to the afternoon when we made love. I doze off after reassuring myself that she will be back. It's not as if I continue to harbour the illusion that I matter a great deal to her. However I do know for sure, she has a connection with her cottage. Regardless of that strange husband of hers and whatever other baggage she may be carrying, it's the place she retreats to when she is hurting.

The stranger within my gate

I should have anticipated it. When I wake up in the morning Samir has disappeared once again after devouring the food I had cooked for him the previous night. He has been a little more responsible this time. He has left me a note.

> *'Sorry. Got to run again. I have to nail this guy who is hell bent on screwing my life. I think I am close to finding the murderer. I will let you know everything once we have trapped the bastard. Take care.*
> *Samir*
> *P.S. What's with the make-up jazz? I want my friend back.*

The postscript makes me furious. With all that is going on in his life, he still does not miss an opportunity to take a dig at me. Besides what's he trying to say? That I should remain frumpy all my life so that he can happily take me for granted? I have no doubt in my mind that the person who is helping him is Vrinda. Why is he trying to be mysterious about it? Do both mother and son take me to be a complete idiot? I am not going to spare him when I meet him next. I have had enough of holding myself captive to some silly vows of childhood friendship. Let me just come across either of them. I am not going to mince words when I give both the mother and son an earful about their slimy ways.

I make myself some breakfast and then sit in the living room, looking outside the window. No one is around. Most cottages in Upper Coonoor are holiday homes now, belonging to the rich and famous of Chennai, Coimbatore and Bangalore. Mrs Kashyap was an exception, like her friend Mrs Sridhar. I wonder vaguely whether I should visit our neighbour and decide against it. She may resent my intrusion. Suddenly a jeep pulls up in front of the cottage and a young man descends from it. I draw my breath in sharply. He looks vaguely familiar.

Is he Nakul? Kabir's dreaded ex, and Sujala's mortal enemy? I can see his profile clearly now, opening the gate. No, he doesn't look anything like the guy I saw in the pictures that I found among Kabir's papers. And yet I feel I have met him somewhere, although for the life of me, I can't recall when and where.

I open the door even before he can ring the bell. 'Good morning,' he greets me with a smile like he has known me all his life. 'I met Mrs Sridhar at the police station. They had asked her to come and sign a statement as she was the last person Mrs Kashyap spoke to. She told me that you were here.'

When I look confused, he grins again, 'You don't recognize me, do you?'

I shake my head. 'Sorry... I know we have met but so much has happened in the past few weeks...' I trail off.

'I am Veer Chaturvedi. I last met you in your flat in Delhi,' he says slowly, waiting for the flicker of recognition to dawn in my eyes.

'I am so sorry,' I feel really embarrassed at that moment. It wasn't very long ago when he had appeared in my doorstep but I had been hung over that morning and since I had left Delhi soon after I had forgotten all about the young policeman who had turned up on a Sunday morning. 'What are you doing here?' I ask, trying to cover up my faux pas.

'Still on the trail of the conspiracy that led to your mother's murder,' he explains. 'I understand you are a friend of the couple who lives here,' the explanation over he looks at me keenly. The smile is back on his face. He seems to be genuinely warming up to me. I find myself responding to his warmth despite my misgivings. It feels good to make human contact, something I crave for all the time in this place.

'Can I get you a cup of hot coffee? It's cold outside, isn't it?' I ask.

'You have forgotten. No tea or coffee for me. Only milk,' his smile broadens into a grin.

'Of course. But this time I must get you your glass of milk,' I smile remembering how flabbergasted I had been when we had met for the first time and he had shared with me how he only drinks milk.

He follows me to the kitchen and stands watching as I heat a glass of milk for him in the microwave and put the kettle to boil to make some tea for me.

'How much sugar?' I ask.

'Two-and-a-half spoons,' he replies, smiling at my startled expression. 'I am a Pahadi. I grew up in Nainital,' he says. As if that piece of information is enough to explain his fetish for milk and two-and-a-half teaspoons of sugar.

We go back to the living room. He insists on carrying the tray that has his glass of milk and my mug of coffee.

'How did you learn about the murders in Coonoor? You are based in Lucknow, aren't you?' I ask.

'We are very well networked nowadays. It's not like the old days,' he answers slowly. There is a pause before he adds 'I told you your mother's death seems to be part of a larger political conspiracy and in cases like this you have no idea how far the trail can go.' A silence comes to rest between us for a few minutes as he slurps down his milk making me feel that whatever the criterion for selecting candidates for the premier police and investigative services in this country, etiquette is not one of them.

But I feel contrite almost immediately afterwards for being such a snob. 'I am sorry. Like I told you that day, I was not feeling very well. So I don't recall much of our conversation. Why did you guys decide to reopen Ma's case?' I ask him.

He looks at me without saying anything for a while. And then he says in a very soft voice as if he is trying to protect me from the impact of his words:

'You must know your mother was a friend of a very influential person in UP.'

Stung by the trouble he is taking to protect the man, I retort, 'That influential person is my father.'

'I am sorry. I was not aware of that fact,' Veer digs into his pocket and brings out a tiny notebook to make a note of this. I notice the clothes he is wearing for the first time. He is in thick, sharply ironed navy blue trousers and a grey shirt, the collar of which is visible over the black, hand-knitted full-sleeved sweater he wears on top. The brown jacket he wore over the sweater when he came in has been taken off and hung on the coat hanger by the door.

Veer spends nearly four hours in the house with me. Once again he asks a lot of questions about my mother and whether she had ever spoken to me about her life being in danger. I tell him about the tiff I had when she had taken me to the bank. When I was in Lucknow, Jamuna had told me how the man had introduced Mother to an astrologer who had predicted that he would win the last election. The same astrologer had warned her that her life could be in danger. I have not been able to share this bit of silly superstition with anyone. Not even Samir. But somehow I feel this strange policeman from UP will understand.

I am right in my assumption. He not only understands but says, 'Everyone in my family believes in astrology. When I was appearing for the Civil Services exam our family astrologer said I would qualify in the first shot and I did.'

I am not aware when we start talking to each other in Hindi, the language I used to speak in only with my mother and Jamuna. I feel completely at ease with Veer, like a friend I have known all my life.

After some time I ask him whether he would like to stay for lunch. He agrees immediately. I am aware everything that is happening between us is rather bizarre. This is not how an officer, however junior, ought to behave. But I am beyond caring. All I know is I am lonely and Veer's company is more than welcome. I have been missing the intimacy I shared with Sujala and Kabir. I won't mind if Veer took me in his arms and made love to me. I chide myself for thinking like a whore who needs rehabilitation.

Once we are in the kitchen Veer insists on taking over and cooking some pulao for the both of us with the few carrots, beans, cauliflower and peas in the fridge. He also makes some sweet tomato chutney to go with it. I try to tempt him with a drink but he refuses. I pour myself one. He looks at me keenly once again. 'An uncle of mine started drinking. It started with a couple of drinks in the evening. Then he started drinking during the day also. We knew his life was ruined after that.' The thing about Veer is that he's a total time-pass. He has an anecdote for every occasion.

'I don't think there is anyone left who is going to care if I ruin my life,' I laugh, trying hard to remove all traces of bitterness from my voice.

'You shouldn't talk like that,' he responds seriously and then referring to the conversation we had earlier asks, 'Don't you want to save your friend?'

'Considering Samir's remarkable talent for showing up at the scene of the crime, I don't think anything or anyone can save him.'

'There is enough evidence to suggest that he had nothing to do with the murder of your mother.'

'Is that right? How did you find that out?' I ask, my heart thudding.

'When he went to see your mother on the day she was

murdered, she was already dead.' So here it comes; the piece of information that Samir has been waiting for, to bail him out of trouble. 'Someone else had gone to visit your mother before your friend entered the house and discovered the dead body. Let's say this person was trying to get away when he heard the door open and so he hid inside. The front door wasn't bolted and the visitor who was in the house saw Samir enter, calling your mother's name. That's what struck me as being odd when we were interrogating this person. Why would Samir call your mother by her name? She was so much older to him. That's just disrespectful.'

'Samir's family is very westernized. They don't believe in addressing others as uncles and aunties however old they might be.' I can't believe I am having this conversation on political correctness, but the news that Samir is innocent has made me less defensive; a lightness suffuses me.

'That's not very nice. We shouldn't blindly ape western culture.'

'I wish you would tell me what my father saw?'

'I don't think I told you who the visitor was?'

'You don't have to say it. It has to be him. I may not have grown up in Lucknow but I was home during the vacations. He is the only one who had a key and the habit of never shutting the door properly after him. Ma used to get irritated with him about that all the time.'

'All these are assumptions you have made. You are rather good at them, you know.' He takes the pan and pours the chutney in a bowl, 'The food is ready to eat now. Even though you may think I am boasting, I must say I cook rather well.'

'Fuck the cooking. Tell me what Samir and my father were doing in her house on the day my mother was murdered.'

'You shouldn't use such language. At least not with someone you have met just twice in your life,' he chides me and then comes to the point, 'Nothing much happened. The visitor saw your friend gasp at the sight of your mother, turn on his heels and run away. If he had stayed and called the police he might have saved himself a lot of trouble and, who knows, perhaps saved the lives of the other victims who were killed after her.'

'How do you know my father didn't kill her?'

'You mean the visitor? I have not given you any names?' Veer sounds so smug when he says this that I feel like slapping him.

'Whatever. Just tell me,' I persist.

'Because your mother was already dead when the visitor came to her house. She had been dead more than three hours. And he was in a meeting at the time she was murdered. More than twenty people can vouch for the fact that he was with them.'

I start laughing.

He looks puzzled. 'What's the matter?'

'Nothing. If my father had any sense he should have told me all this a long time ago. Even the other day when I called...' I choke and desperately try to blink back my tears. What's the point? Ever since I have been old enough to understand, neither Ma nor I have been that important to him.

Veer and I eat in silence. He stands watching as I clear the plates and do the dishes. I guess he is the typical Indian male trying to be modern. He can pitch in with the cooking, but it would never occur to him to clean up afterwards. That always has to be a woman's job.

'When did you decide he was your father? Did your mother tell you that?' Veer asks suddenly.

'Nobody had to tell me. I always knew he was my father,' I snap at him.

He flinches and looks away.

Veer stays for a week and drops in frequently. He says he is tired of the Madrasis and eating only idli sambar, that is made for him in the guest-house. In the cold weather, he craves aloo ka paranthas for breakfast. Since he feels at ease with me because of our shared origins, he comes over frequently because he can cook and eat the food he enjoys. At least that's his excuse. At times I feel there is something more to his visits. Maybe he thinks he can unearth some more information from me. But despite not trusting him fully, I am glad for the company he provides.

He shares all the latest gossip from Lucknow and tells me fascinating stories about the politicians and high-ranking officials in the state. About their perversions and their faith in tantriks. Veer is a great storyteller and the little flourishes he adds in Hindi make me laugh after a long time.

When he comes to meet me for the last time before he leaves for Lucknow, he tells me his stay has been quite useless professionally but, personally, he is happy to have made a new friend. He also tells me he will write me a letter from Lucknow.

A couple of days after Veer leaves, something he had mentioned when he came to meet me the first time in Coonoor comes back to haunt me. A fever takes hold of me for nearly a week and the nights are so bad I end up feeling I would be better off dead.

I have a voracious appetite once I recover. I cook myself large meals. I go for long walks and on my way back stop over at Mrs Sridhar's house for tea. We are friends now. She tells me she also went to boarding school. Except the school she went to sounds unreal and straight out of the pages of an Enid Blyton book. If I ask her too many questions about her school days she gets annoyed. She doesn't like talking about her friend Mrs Kashyap and her murder. Maybe it's like that with the old. They don't wish to be reminded of their mortality. She asks me one day how long I intend staying in her town. I tell her I don't know.

She looks at me and smiles, 'I guess you can't leave until your hosts return.'

She is right. Ever since Veer left, I have been meaning to get back to Lucknow. I have to meet the man and ask him something. I can also do this over the phone but I feel this particular confrontation will work much better in person. So that he is not prepared and is forced to give me the answer I am looking for. I know I am being foolish. There is no reason why he would want to conceal anything. For all I know he may be shocked at what I have assumed all along. It's funny how difficult it is for us to shake off a reality we have created for ourselves. I seem to be an expert in this area. My fantasies have shaped my world.

This was true when I was a child. This is true when I am all of twenty-six.

After all, how easily I have transformed an afternoon of lust into a lifetime of longing.

She has not bothered to call or write to me after they left. But I have foolishly convinced myself we have a future together.

For I have known agony...

A week after he left, I receive a letter from Veer Chaturvedi. The last time I received letters by snail mail was when I was in school and got Mother's fortnightly missives. The world changed in the last decade and now it's all emails, SMSs and phone calls. I take it out of the letter-box and smell it gingerly. The envelope and the handmade paper on which the letter is written emit a faint fragrance; as if they have been sprayed with perfume.

Dear Neha,

Believe you me I am as surprised to find myself writing this letter, as you must be about receiving it. I never thought something like this is going to happen to me especially when I was on official duty, even though I have to admit this is not a very important case. They have just bowed to political pressure and delegated the case to a junior officer like me.

I have not mentioned my age to you. I am going to turn 29 in February. Three months from now. My mother has been trying to get me married for the last four years. But I have always told her 'Mein aap ka eklota beta hoon, mujhe kisi bhi gai ke khoonte se band doge kya?' That is not to say I think women are cows. Ha! Ha!

Coming to more serious matters, I think I love you and want to get married to you. This whole thing happened like how it happens in films. I fell in love with you as soon as I saw you for the first time while you were thinking I was a salesman. Your family background is of no concern to me. Although I come from a traditional family, we are not conservative in a bad way. My grandfather, Ram Prakash Chaturvedi was a freedom fighter and despite societal opposition, he married a widow, Chanda Rani.

The facts pertaining to your late mother are a bit unfortunate but I know you have a very good character and you will be a good wife.

Please don't be in a hurry to give your decision. These are matters of life and death and I will understand if you take your time. Once you agree, I will take up this matter with my family.

I miss you very much.
Yours faithfully,
Veer Chaturvedi
IPS

I start to cry after reading the letter. I wonder what Veer would think of me if he knew my past. I wish I could be with my mother and Samir and show it to them. How all of us would have laughed. As it stands, I feel alone, adrift and depressed.

They come back just as suddenly as they had left. Kabir wears lines of unhappiness on his forehead. As for her, she has wrapped herself in a coldness I cannot penetrate. I can no longer predict what she is thinking. Not that I really ever could. But there were times I knew she was going to smile and make me feel on top of the world; something that she rarely does after she has come back from wherever they disappeared to.

Neither of them have much to say to me. I am sure if I announce I want to leave the cottage and the town there is not going to be a murmur of protest from either of them. But I am angry and don't want to let them off the hook so easily. The way they take me for granted makes me feel I have been used and what hurts more is I don't even know their reason for doing so. She has taken to playing the devoted wife to Kabir. Looking at them, one would think they are brand ambassadors for the grand Indian marriage. After all that Samir has told me, I want to puke at the deception they are trying to practice on the world.

She brings it up a couple of days later. It is almost evening and Kabir has stepped out to buy groceries. It has been sunny all day yet my head feels heavy. As if something bad is going to happen and I can't do anything to prevent it. We are sitting in the living room as far away from each other as possible. She had flinched when I had tried to hug her on her return. I have maintained a distance with her ever since.

'What are your plans, Neha?' Posing the question has not been easy for her; she looks away carefully as if not wanting to see my reaction.

'Is that a polite way of informing me that I am no longer welcome in your house?' I am sure she senses the deliberate challenge in my voice.

I have underestimated her. She seems as prepared for combat as I am: 'Even if you plan to stay on in Coonoor, have you done anything about looking for a house? That was the original plan, right?'

'The person who was meant to help me house-hunt was murdered.'

She draws her breath in sharply. 'What are you talking about?'

'Mrs Kashyap. She was murdered. Just like my mother and your friend Karla.'

'There has been another murder. Why didn't you tell us?'

'Have you had any time for me since you came back? You have been too busy playing happy family with your husband.'

'I am happy,' she says. 'Happier than I have ever been.'

'Because Mrs Kashyap has been murdered?' I know I am being plain nasty but my anger has made me give up any pretence of civility.

'Don't be silly. I had no time for that busybody when I was living with Samir, just like I have no patience with our neighbour, your new friend. But that doesn't mean I wanted her to be murdered.'

So she has noticed things about me after she has come back. For some strange reason that makes me feel good. But I also know I can't allow myself to get swept away again.

'Samir came here one night. He was looking for the painting.'

'What do you mean he was looking for the painting? He is the one who has it,' she retorts angrily.

'Not anymore.'

'Well then, it's just like Samir not to hold on to anything that's important,' she says contemptuously.

I am not going to let her get away that easily. 'How could you do what you did to him?'

'Do what?' She manages to look puzzled and concerned at the same time.

'You just don't care about anyone or anything, do you? You enjoy hurting people.'

'Stop being so dramatic.'

'But it's your life that is full of drama.' I am no longer worried about the consequences of what I am saying. The way she widens her eyes tells me the barb has hit home.

'So Samir has filled you in with all the details of my life? Losers. Both of you,' she spits out, getting up to go.

'So we are all losers?' I can't resist asking.

'Yes,' she's equally relentless.

'Does that apply to Chetna and Nakul too?'

'Oh, so he has told you about them, ' she turns and shakes her head slowly as she sits down again.

'He had to warn me. I am his best friend,' I am not losing any opportunity to be unpleasant.

'Why aren't you staying in his cottage then?' she counters snidely.

'You know very well why I stayed here. You made me.'

'Don't be stupid. Did Kabir or I drug you and bring you here kicking and screaming? You came here because you wanted to. Because you were stupid enough to believe that you could be more important to me than Kabir. Samir made the same mistake.'

I desperately wrack my memory. Have I ever confessed to her in a vulnerable moment that this is what I had wanted all along?

She smiles sensing my confusion. 'So I am right. That's what you wanted all along. Based on what? That one afternoon when I had wanted to punish him for whispering Nakul's name when he was making love to me?'

I find my face going red. I have relived that afternoon many times. But to have it mentioned in such a callous fashion by her destroys everything that I have held precious about the two of us.

'Listen, Neha,' her voice softens suddenly. 'It's not as if I don't understand. What it is to love and not be loved.'

'If by that you mean how much you love Kabir, I don't believe you,' I retort sullenly.

'Why? Because I made love to you while he was watching?'

'I don't want you to talk about that.'

'What else can we talk about? You seem to be fixated on that one afternoon. It's as if whatever happened afterwards between us does not matter at all. I have tried so hard to make up for having used you that afternoon. And it's not as if you didn't get anything out of it...'

'Maybe because that's the only time you have been honest with me.' I don't know whether the words are for her benefit or mine.

'Strange how much like Chetna you sound when you say that.'

'Do I? Perhaps because she is also someone you have used and discarded.'

She laughs again. 'Your thinking is so distorted. Just like your notions about love. You decided you were in love with me. Did I once say I reciprocated your feelings?'

Everything she has said until then has given me no space to enter and I have had to fall back on cheap repartee to counter them. Finally there is an opportunity to tell her what I have wanted to all along.

'It's not about words. It's about who you really are and what you want. You can never be happy with a man.'

'How do you know that? How does anyone know that? I believed that too. For a long time, I believed that because right from the time I was in school no man could arouse me. There was the mandatory boyfriend in high school and after that in university. There were other girls before Chetna came into my life. Chetna and I thought we were special,' she pauses to collect her thoughts. 'We thought we will grow old together. The weddings were their idea. I was dead against them. But they were angry with me for being a spoilsport.'

She gets up and goes to the kitchen. When she comes back she has a glass of sherry in her hand. 'You have to forgive me. I can't do this without alcohol. Shall I fix you a drink?'

'No thanks. I don't want to be lulled once again into believing something that isn't true.'

She shakes her head, smiling. 'If you could only hear how ridiculous you sound.'

Unexpected tears sting my eyes. She has the grace to look ashamed. 'Look, I never meant to hurt any of you.

Not you or your friend Samir. Or for that matter, Nakul or Chetna. I used to think Kabir was a bore. I tolerated him only because of Chetna. And then when we were forced to be with each other on that ridiculous honeymoon, we drank a lot of wine one night and we made love. It wasn't even satisfactory. But the next morning when I woke up, a thin stream of dust motes had made its way through an opening in the window. It bathed him in an orange glow as he snored gently, and something felt right. More than it ever had. I knew we were meant to be together. This whole notion of love or for that matter sexuality being this loud dramatic thing is something we have to blame poets and writers for. When you experience the real thing you know it is as unobtrusive as it can get. Even Kabir doesn't understand it sometimes. That's why he chose to go back with Nakul when he came and created all that drama here. Because Kabir asked me to, I tried to live with Chetna again. But in less than a month both of us knew it wasn't going to work. We women are smarter that way. What was lost was lost. So I came back to the only place I have ever been really happy. Because I had lived with him in this cottage. I didn't hope to have him back. And this house without him turned unbearable. I was just so lost...' her voice trails off.

'You needn't have despaired. Kabir followed you after a few months...' I add what she has left out.

'You understand more than you are willing to concede.' Her voice softens, 'It was in the interim period that Samir and Karla happened. I wasn't thinking those days. I just wanted to forget, and anyone who could help me forget the pain for sometime was welcome. Sex is such a great antidote to depression. Except the relief doesn't last for long.' The rueful smile is back on her face.

'What about me? The two of you were together at that time. You were not pining for him then.' I can't recognize my own voice when I ask her this. I sound like a beggar seeking alms.

'Both of us regret what happened with you. We like you. We didn't want to hurt you. It was just one afternoon of getting even with each other. It could have been anyone,' she says gently.

I get up and run out blindly as she comes after me calling my name. I almost collide with Kabir who has just entered through the gate, his hands laden with shopping bags.

'Kabir, stop her!' I can hear her yelling behind me. But I am out of the house, running, aware that it is cold, aware that my tears feel curiously warm, aware that things are never going to be the same.

It's all over as far as I am concerned.

I don't know how long I run. I am on this deserted road near the club and a car whizzes past. It slows down a few metres ahead and stops for me to reach it. A voice calls out from within, 'Is that you, Neha? What are you doing here?'

It is Randeep.

I stand there, shivering, looking foolishly at the car as he comes out. There is nothing I can do to avoid him. Despite the fact that I am distraught, I can still worry whether he can make out from the tearstains on my cheeks that I have been crying. I cover my face with my hands, acting as if I can't bear the cold.

'Don't try to pretend you have been jogging. The clothes you are wearing are all wrong,' he says smiling at me.

For a moment, I am tempted to protest and lie to him that the jeans, T shirt and the pullover I am wearing are my standard jogging gear. I am wearing sneakers on my feet after all. But before I can say anything, he opens the door and asks me to get in. I hesitate for just a moment before I accept his invitation. How does it matter? How does anything matter anymore?

I am sure he will take me to the club but instead he drives to the hotel I had stayed in. He heads to the coffee shop with me following him meekly. When the waiter comes to our table, he asks for two strong coffees.

'What are you doing here?' The question is not unexpected.

'I don't know,' I answer. I don't think there is a need to be anything but honest with him. I really don't know what I am doing in this place. My excuse for coming to Coonoor was that I was trying to find my mother's murderer. But deep down I always knew I had come back seeking her, hoping for the impossible. This is something he will never understand.

'How long have you been here?' he asks, appraising me shrewdly. I have read somewhere that you can gauge by a person's demeanour how long she has been staying in a place. It is quite pointless to lie to him anyway.

'It's been over two months, I think.'

'Does Vrinda know?'

'I never told her. But Samir may have…'

'Samir? But he is… When did you meet him?' I am aware his voice has turned cold. Mother and son are now keeping things from him too. I wonder how he feels about that.

'Nearly a month back. He came looking for that painting of Sujala's that went missing from his house. And then he also spent the night at Sujala's cottage on the day Mrs Kashyap was murdered...'

'So you've been staying in that woman's house. For how long?' The impatience is evident in his voice.

'Almost a couple of months.'

'And were they also there when Samir came over?' I can sense something different in his voice when he asks me that. Something that tells me he is very angry about the whole thing.

'No. They had gone back to the US when he barged in like that. There was no one in the house apart from me,' I wonder whether Randeep and I have a similar story to share. He may have been used by Samir and Vrinda just like I have been used by Sujala and Kabir.

'And what did Samir tell you when he met you?'

'He told me about the time he was with Sujala. What happened between the two of them?'

'Did he tell you anything about his present whereabouts?'

'He went away before I could ask him that. All he would say was someone was helping him. I assumed it was Vrinda. And yes, he did mention you have also been very supportive after Karla's death.'

'Did he say anything specific about the person who was helping him?' The way he is shooting questions at me, I may as well be being interrogated by the police.

'No, he didn't tell me about anyone in particular. But it has to be Vrinda, right? Who else can it be? Don't tell me you don't know anything about all this?' I am getting tired of all the concealments and subterfuge. Can't people be honest with me for a change?

'No,' he says slowly. 'A lot of things have been kept from me.'

The waiter brings our coffee and that gives him time to mull over things. 'Why don't you come over to Samir's cottage tomorrow by noon? I will get Vrinda with me. We had better get to the bottom of this. You do understand, don't you, how I feel? What it is to be kept in the dark? It seems as if they do this to me all the time. I am always the outsider.'

'If there is anything that I can understand at this point of time in my life, it is how it feels to be kept in the dark and to be treated like an outsider,' I respond tiredly.

'Then you must also understand why I don't want you to mention any of this to anyone. Not even to the friends you are staying with.' He shakes his head regretfully. 'I find it difficult to trust anyone anymore.'

It as if he is giving words to what I have been feeling ever since their return.

They are waiting for me in the living room. Kabir opens the door as soon as I get inside the house. They must have heard Randeep's car.

'Thank god you are safe,' Sujala remarks as soon he closes the door after letting me in.

'Really? I must say you are always surprising me with your concern,' I find it difficult to keep the sarcasm out of my voice.

'Stop it, Neha. We are dealing with a tragedy here. Everything can't always revolve around you. And it was my idea to ask you to leave. So that we have the space to grieve,' I have never heard Kabir so angry. Hurt and confused I turn towards him only to hear her say, 'It's okay. She doesn't know.'

'I don't know what?' I am no longer shocked about the fact that there could be something else she has kept away from me.

'Nakul is dead,' she says calmly. 'We didn't give you the details before we left. But that was because even we didn't know how serious it was at that time. Also we didn't know you were aware of his existence.'

'Dead? When? How? I thought he was in India.'

'Now why should you think that? Nakul was rushed to the hospital a month ago. He had a new partner, Daniel. According to him, Nakul had been complaining of a recurring headache for some time. He didn't take it very seriously. Just popped some aspirin when it came on. When he fainted one evening, Daniel rushed him to the hospital. They discovered a tumour in his brain. Before they could operate, he was dead.'

'You could have told me before you left,' I know I am being unreasonable after she has explained what kept them from telling me.

'Like I told you, we didn't know how serious it was. Chetna had called Kabir to inform him Nakul had been hospitalized. By the time we reached, it was too late,' she says all this tonelessly as if she was reading it from a newspaper.

There is a silence after that and the three of us look at each other. I am the first to grow uncomfortable and blurt out, 'I am leaving tomorrow. I need to pack.'

They leave the room together but at the door it is Kabir who turns and apologizes for all that has happened. I ask him not to worry and say that I am thankful to them for letting me stay with them at such a difficult time in my life. I am hoping against hope that she will come back to the room and take me in her arms one last time.

But all I can hear are her footsteps as she climbs the stairs.

The colour of Kurinji

O nce again I am unable to sleep. My ears strain to catch any sound from the room upstairs, but everything is still. They seem to have gone to sleep without much trouble after letting me know that I was no more than a pawn in their sexual politics. So many things have happened in the last one year that I am unable to muster either rage or grief. I toss and turn the whole night, hoping the day would break, hoping the sun would shine, hoping I can escape somewhere so that I can remove all traces of the time I have spent in this house and in this town. I am not coming back. Not even for Mother's sake.

I doze off listening to the birds chirping at dawn. I am woken by a knock on the door. Kabir has brought up a tray with my morning tea and some cookies. He has never done this before. Maybe it's his way of making me feel welcome on what is going to be my last day in his house. Or perhaps they are worried about my sleeping so late. I am usually up and about by the time they wake up. Or it could be that he has come to find out whether I am okay after the hurt and despair his wife has subjected me to.

Who cares why he has decided to be so thoughtful at the fag end of it. None of it matters. Not anymore.

'Good morning,' he smiles. The kindness I used to sense in him when we first met is back in his demeanour.

'Good morning,' I respond, desperately trying to sound cheerful. He starts to leave after placing the tray on my bedside table. I call out to him. He turns and looks at me searchingly. 'What is it?' he asks, growing increasingly uncomfortable as I struggle to find the right words.

'How easy is it for you? I mean how do you manage with her?'

He looks puzzled at first until realization dawns in his eyes gradually. 'It was never easy. At first I thought if I played along, she would come to see the futility of it. I felt I had a responsibility towards Chetna. You have not met my friend...' he trails off.

'I know about Chetna. I know about them,' I am surprised at how calm I sound.

'Initially I thought if I was not so resistant to the idea, Sujala would drop it. After all, resistance always makes all the forbidden things much more attractive. I convinced myself that if I agreed to her suggestion of running away and hiding from them, she would see how silly it was after some time and we could go back and pretend it was all a joke. We were always pulling pranks on each other even though Nakul used to be livid if he was at the receiving end,' he pauses once again to collect his thoughts. He is not aware that Sujala has come to the door and is listening to our conversation. He continues to explain:

'It's only when we came here and started living together that I learnt how much I needed the same things as her.

Maybe I had known all along that there was no going back. I loved Nakul but it was hard to live with all his tantrums and rages. With her there was such a sense of ease. Also, after a disastrous first experience, I never thought I could make love to a woman but with her I discovered it was possible. It may not have been…' he realizes he is giving too much away and shakes his head. 'Anyway, this is my life now and I am happy with it,' he says and turns to see his wife crying quietly. He goes towards her and gently guides her out of my room.

I tell them I don't need any breakfast, that I don't feel like it and that I am going out for lunch. I call the travel agents to inform them that I would like to take a flight from Coimbatore to Delhi the next day. They agree to send me an e-ticket if I make an online payment. I am determined to appear cheerful. I have promised myself I am not going to meet Kabir and Sujala ever again in my life. Once I get back to Lucknow, I am going to have a chat with the man and afterwards I am going to get a job. Preferably in some other country.

There is one last conversation I need to have in this place and that is with Vrinda and Randeep. I need to confront Vrinda so that she knows she can't play with the lives of others in order to protect her son. I am going to leave it to her to communicate to Samir about my departure from Coonoor. I am sure they are in touch with each other. I tried to call him in the morning but his phone was switched off.

It's getting on to half past eleven when I set out for Samir's cottage. I try to soak in all the sights on the way.

I am bidding farewell to the town. I don't know whether I want to hold on to the memories of the people I have met here but the landscape is a different matter altogether. I have always loved the charm and solitude of this quaint town. When I reach Samir's cottage, I walk towards the Kurinji bushes and stand marvelling at them.

I see that Randeep has come to the front door and is getting impatient at my dawdling. I am reminded of the first morning I had spent in Samir's cottage after being summoned by Vrinda. I had come and stood in the same spot and the nosy Mrs Kashyap had peered over her wall. She is dead now at the hands of a savage murderer. It's all a bit overwhelming.

I turn and walk towards the cottage. Randeep follows me to the living room and closes the door behind him. I look around for Vrinda. Randeep appears to be very still. He is probably tense about his ensuing confrontation with his wife in the presence of a third person. I turn and look at him, the unspoken question hanging in the air.

'Vrinda was here. But you know her. She suddenly remembered she had to send a fax to her Shanghai office and rushed to the club to do it. She should be back any minute.'

I sit down not knowing what to say. Randeep is looking keenly at me. 'Should I get you some coffee? I have just put the kettle on.'

'Thank you,' I tell him. 'I can do with some caffeine in my system.'

'Hmm... so you are ready to poison yourself?' he jokes and goes inside the kitchen. Something doesn't feel right about the way he says that. I don't know why but I feel there is something unpleasant lingering in the cottage. Like the smell of a dead rodent in a room that has been locked up for a long time. It is all pervasive.

When Randeep comes back with a tray I tell him about the way I feel.

He looks confused. 'Now, why on earth would you find this cottage anything but welcoming? You have spent so many happy and carefree days here with Samir.'

'I don't know. I just do. Are you sure Vrinda said she will be here soon?' I ask.

'Of course,' he reassures me, 'Don't worry, she will be here anytime now.'

The piping hot coffee feels good after the walk in the chilly weather although there is a strange aftertaste. I notice he hasn't touched his cup.

'Why aren't you having your coffee? I thought you were craving for it.'

'I prefer to drink it after it has cooled down a bit.'

'Really? But you finished your cup in no time when we were in the restaurant yesterday.'

He senses the bafflement in my voice and laughs out aloud. My eyes are blurring and all of a sudden his face has multiplied into three. All three of them are sneering at me. 'The trouble is you notice too many things,' they say quietly. 'But you won't after today, I promise.' Their silent laugh has turned into a muted guffaw. I am experiencing a pain that I have never felt before. My head is threatening to split and my stomach is ready to burst any moment. I shut my eyes tight. I am back in the garden, marvelling at the Kurinji bushes. Drops of blood spill from my palms, turning them red. I try to get up and collapse on the spot.

Randeep is coming towards me with the rope I had last seen in Samir's studio. When was that? I can't remember. The pain is unbearable now. I am trying to scream but my voice fails me. I can hear someone knocking furiously at the door. I hear shouts but they may as well be the noises in my head.

Randeep stops near me looking puzzled. I hear a loud crash just before everything blurs and fades into an inky blackness.

I have died and despite not having done too many good deeds in my lifetime I have been transported to heaven. It has to be heaven because whenever I open my eyes with difficulty, and it takes a Herculean effort to do so, I find everything around me is in pristine white. There is a persistent, intoxicating fragrance that feels familiar too. I am not sure how long I stay in this celestial world.

One day I feel a hand on my forehead and hear a familiar voice that says, 'There is no fever today, thankfully.' I open my eyes slowly, blinking furiously at the brightness. A hazy shape takes human form. I recognize Vrinda. She smiles faintly at me. It feels all wrong. They have yanked me out of my heaven. I am lying intubated on a hospital bed, and surrounding it are Vrinda, Samir and Veer Chaturvedi. The first thought that takes hold of me is that it is Samir who has had an accident and he is in hospital. I turn confused eyes towards him.

'It's all right. The bastard couldn't get you after all,' he declares. Vrinda flinches when she hears this. Veer waves at me. Suddenly a policeman appears beside him and whispers something to him. He leaves the room leaving me alone with mother and son. 'I am sorry, Neha,' Vrinda says in a small voice. 'You lost Ratna because of us.' Samir moves to her side to comfort her. And I find the numbing heaviness sweep over me again. Just before I succumb to the blissful darkness, I manage to whisper, 'I was such a fool. I walked right into the trap he laid for me.'

Two weeks later, when I have recovered enough to sit up in bed, they fill me in with the bits and pieces. Veer is the one who cracked the case and he explains most of it to me.

Randeep did not know my mother until he got in touch with her on Vrinda's behalf for expanding their business interests. Their relationship would have stayed at a professional level if Randeep hadn't found out that Mother had an agent working for her who did background checks on whomever she was doing business with. This agent had accidently stumbled on the mysterious death of Randeep's child and found out that his first wife had left him because she felt Randeep had something to do with the death of the child. She too had died a year later in a driving accident. No one had suspected Randeep of having a hand in her fatal accident at that time although they were reopening the probe to find out whether he had played a part in that too, ever since he had been caught red-handed trying to kill me.

My mother thrived on information of the kind that she had uncovered on Randeep. It gave her a sense of power over those she was dealing with. She may not have brought up what she knew when Vrinda and he came home for dinner. But she is likely to have played some mind games with him when he met her again on his own.

Like all psychopaths who want their private lives to remain private, the digging of his past had made Randeep both anxious and angry. He may not have been sure how much she had found out. And the uncertainty made him feel she was better off dead. When he learnt Samir was going to meet Mother, he realized he had a golden opportunity to implicate his stepson in the crime he was going to commit. Samir had mentioned to Randeep that he was going to Lucknow to seek Mother's help to locate Sujala when Randeep and he had an argument about Samir's personal life impacting Vrinda's health. So Randeep decided to kill two birds with one stone and timed her murder in such a way that Samir would be the one to discover her body. Since he knew about his stepson's fragile state of mind, he hoped the discovery of the dead body would devastate Samir, and even if he wasn't arrested for the murder immediately, he would do something foolish to attract the suspicions of those probing the murder. What he hadn't bargained for was that Samir would be able to keep his wits about him and flee from the scene of crime. Since he failed in his mission to make Samir pay for the sins of omission and sins of commission he blamed him for the first time, he bumped off Karla and then Mrs Kashyap in order to make the world believe Samir was a serial-killer and the frustration he had suffered with Sujala, who had thwarted his love, had made him go on a rampage. Because he didn't get his way the first time and Samir managed to escape, it became an obsession with him to ensure Samir found himself behind bars for multiple murders.

'But why did he hate Samir so much that he was willing to go to the trouble of murdering two innocent women in addition to Mother?' I ask. None of it is making sense to me anymore.

'He has clammed up and is not talking. He is too clever to confess to anything. The same high-profile lawyer he had engaged for Samir is representing him. All I can say is that maybe his first marriage and the death of his child hold some answers to the bits we can't explain,' Veer sums up.

'I am sorry, but even though he tried to kill me, I find it difficult to believe he was such an evil man,' I murmur feebly.

'Surprisingly, maybe because I never knew him, I have had no difficulty in believing he murdered all the three women, including your mother,' Veer continues. 'He was the only one present when his child fell from the fourth-floor terrace of his ancestral house. His first wife blamed him for taking the child to the terrace.'

Veer informs me he has managed to track the younger sister of Randeep's first wife in Australia and according to her, her sister had once confided in her that Randeep resented his own son and she had grown to be afraid of him. He was extremely possessive about her and once the child came he would quarrel with her often, accusing her of neglecting him.

'I can't believe he murdered his own son,' I interrupt, feeling slightly sick in my stomach.

'Well, no one believed it at that time. And whatever his poor wife had to say was also dismissed as the after-effects arising from the shock of losing her son. But now we have also found out that Randeep had a younger brother and he drowned in the house pool when the two of them were children. They were swimming and their nanny was supervising them. She went to use the restroom and when she came back, Randeep's younger brother was dead. The blame fell on her and Randeep's parents were advised to move to another country to help him get over the trauma. So they moved to London for a few years. I think the evil was present in him all along.'

Veer's explanations are substantiated by Samir when he drops into the hospital a few days later. 'I was not imagining things about him like you always used to tell me. I started staying away from Mother and him because he used to make me uncomfortable. Especially, when he saw Mum and me together. I went to Paris for a few years and he must have thought I was out of their lives. But then I came back and the entire fiasco with Sujala happened. Mother got obsessed with helping me and all his old demons resurfaced.'

I wonder how easy it has been for Samir to come to terms with all this. Imagine having a stepfather who hates you so much that he is willing to murder innocents brutally only so that the world can condemn his stepson for being a serial-killer.

When I put all the strands together, I realize Randeep must have been behind Samir's accident too. If Samir had died in that accident, it would have been easy for the police to conclude that the young man, disturbed by the two murders he had committed, had gone off the edge. It was when Samir was recuperating in Coimbatore that Randeep suggested that he move to his plantation just outside Coonoor. He convinced Vrinda that Samir was in danger and needed to be in a safe place. He assured both of them that the arrangement was going to last until such time they could track the real killer. As for Samir, by that time, he must have been desperate to cling to any straws that came his way. In any case, he was not able to think rationally after the trauma of being arrested for a murder he didn't commit. Besides, he had believed all along that it was Nakul who was murdering all the women and trying to pin the blame on Samir.

'All along I believed that the creep was the murderer. He had attacked me once. I told you he came across as quite unhinged and it wasn't difficult for me to conclude that in his twisted mind he thought Kabir had come back for me and not Sujala and he wanted to punish me.'

Samir stops when he sees me shaking my head and smiling. 'What's the matter?' the irritation is evident in his voice.

'Do you know the poor guy is dead?' I tell Samir. 'He had a brain tumour. Maybe that is what caused him to react strangely at times. Kabir and Sujala went back when they were told by Chetna that he had been admitted to the hospital. He was dead within a day.'

'I am sorry to hear that. But he managed to psych me good and proper the couple of times we met.'

I don't know whether it's our inability to deal with the intensity of what we have been discussing, but both of us start to giggle together. 'It's just that some of it sounds so absurd, almost funny, in retrospect. You seem to attract all types of psychos in your life,' I try to explain why I am behaving so badly after talking about someone's untimely death.

'You are in no position to comment on psychos, since you are one too,' Samir says, and joins in the laughter.

Samir also shares with me that on the night he had come to take the painting from Sujala's house, he had told Randeep he was going back to live in his own cottage. 'I was not able to paint on the plantation. You know I can start a painting anywhere, but I need to come back to my studio to give it the finishing touches. I told him I needed to get back to my place for at least a couple of days and he agreed. He must have planned Mrs Kashyap's murder to time it with my stay in the cottage. I saw the body and freaked out. Everything went smoothly according to his plan. But what he didn't know was that I had met you before I went back to my cottage. He didn't know that you had come back to Coonoor and were staying in Sujala's house. It must have come as a shock to him that we had met and had a long conversation. He wasn't sure what I had shared with you. And then he learnt I also met you on the day Mrs Kashyap was murdered. Maybe he thought you will start suspecting him once you knew he was behind my disappearance. He's really twisted and it's not easy to understand all his motivations.'

'Why didn't you tell him that you had met me?'

'It wasn't intentional. I didn't meet him after the first time I met you in Sujala's house. And then the shock of seeing a third dead body was too much for me. I almost started believing I was committing the murders when I was not in my senses. Randeep had thoughtfully stacked the plantation library with books on the psychology of serial killers. So it didn't seem like a priority at that time to share with him that I had met you. But by that time he must have been losing it completely. Everything that was kept away from him must have felt like a conspiracy to him.'

'What happened to the painting?' I ask.

'It's back in my studio. I think Randeep flicked it initially and then brought it back afterwards. I can only speculate about his intention for stealing the painting since he isn't talking. Maybe he was looking forward to placing it strategically next to your dead body to convince the cops that I was this sick, demented artist,' Samir says and turns contrite immediately for talking about the attack on me in such a callous fashion. 'I am sorry. That was insensitive of me,' he apologizes.

I think of Mother and why she let Randeep inside the house on the day he killed her even after she had done a background check on him. But she had never been afraid of anything or anyone. Maybe he had just surprised her by dropping in unannounced. Maybe, when Vrinda and he had come over for dinner to her place, she had let it slip that Jamuna was going to be on leave for a couple of weeks to visit her village. He must have seized the opportunity. The troubling realization comes to haunt me that I have allowed the man who murdered my mother to buy me dinner barely a year later. Bile rises up my throat and I start to cough.

'Easy, Neha,' Veer says, coming into the room. He turns to Samir reproachfully. 'You shouldn't make her talk so much.' He turns to me and explains, 'The doctors have still not been able to figure out what he had put in your coffee. It seems like a small quantity of some kind of native poison that the locals make. Not enough to kill you but enough to cripple you for nearly a week and cause you so much pain.'

I look at both of them, standing side by side. 'It's over now, isn't it? That's what matters, don't you think?' I tell them brightly.

When they nod their heads in agreement, it seems as if they have been rehearsing their movements to get them perfectly synchronized.

Let's heal now

Vrinda drops in one evening. In her usual efficient way, she ensures that she gets some time alone with me. I am not surprised by anything she has to say. The crux of it being that she never suspected that the man she had married could turn out to be such a monster. She is very worried that the media might get hold of the story and ruin her life as well as Samir's. I don't quite know how to react when she starts to cry after sharing her apprehensions. But I learn something new about Samir and Vrinda that day. It's always going to be about them. The fact that I lost my mother because of the man she chose to marry is incidental to her in the larger scheme of the tragedy she sees engulfing her and her beloved son.

After she leaves, I realize something good has come out of all this nasty business. I am gaining fresh perspectives on life and living. I start missing my mother a lot. I wish I hadn't been so rough with her when she was alive. That I had gone along on the shopping expeditions she was always trying to drag me to; that I had told her how much I loved it when, without there being an occasion for it, she would cook my favourite dishes for me, when I was a child; that I had shared with her how jealous I felt when we went out together after I had grown up and I could feel the eyes of men on her. It's too late now for any of that.

Sujala and Kabir also drop in once during visiting hours – their only visit in the two months I spend convalescing. Thankfully Samir is not around when they stop by. Otherwise it would have been so awkward for all of us. Kabir is mostly silent while she chatters nineteen to the dozen. She tells me they were worried to death when I didn't turn up that night, even after it turned dark on the day I left their cottage. They called the police and the man at the station asked them to come over the next morning if I didn't turn up at night and file a missing person complaint. They had checked with Mrs Sridhar but she didn't know anything, either. She had not been keeping well ever since her friend had died and hardly ventured outdoors. But she did put them through a grilling session, accusing them of causing harm to me. Later that night Veer had visited them personally to inform them that I was in hospital and he would let them know when they could visit me. When they had pressed him for more information, he told them about how Randeep had tried to kill me.

'It confused us at that time, but when Veer called again to tell us we can visit you, we managed to get the entire story from him,' she informs me brightly.

'She means she managed to get it out of him. You know how persuasive she can be. I had nothing to do with it,' Kabir interjects.

'I know,' I tell him and we smile at each other.

They leave soon after that, promising to drop in again. But something tells me they won't be coming back.

It doesn't matter anymore.

I feel nothing for her any more.

After they leave, Veer comes bustling into the room. 'She is a *very* nice lady. It's difficult to believe she started living with Samir just because her husband left the country for a few months.'

I look out of the window. There are some things that are best kept from Veer. He wouldn't be able to handle them.

'Tell me, how did you zero in on Randeep?' I ask in order to change the topic.

'That was not so difficult. We always suspect a person who is either close to the victim or close to the person against whom there is plenty of evidence but no clear motive. And we get especially suspicious if the evidence keeps piling against one individual, as was happening in the case of your friend. It didn't take me long to figure out that someone was trying to frame him.'

'You are very clever.' I can't believe I am complimenting Veer like this. But the flattery works, making him open up even more.

'You know, I never went back to Lucknow after the week I spent with you in Coonoor. I lied to you about that,' he confesses with a sheepish smile. 'I stayed back and all the time I was shadowing that man. I had followed him to the plantation where your friend was hiding. I told you I had found out in Lucknow that your friend had reached your mother's house after she was murdered. So he was never really a suspect. I knew somebody was committing the murders and trying to frame your friend. It had to be the stepfather.'

I wonder why Veer never refers to Samir by his name in his absence. He is always talking about Samir as 'my friend'. Maybe he is jealous of Samir. Like all my boyfriends have been in the past. But I find it sweet that he is so transparent about his feelings.

'But what about the letter you wrote me from Lucknow?' I ask.

'I wrote and posted it from Ooty. I didn't think you would check the postmark,' he confesses shamelessly.

That gets me a little mad and I decide to test him further.

'Why did you wait for him to drug me, before you broke in?' I try to sound stern when I say that.

'Well, I was peering through the window and couldn't hear a word. I only realized what had happened when you collapsed after having the coffee.'

'You mean to say you were observing us all the time and waited until I was almost killed?' I accuse him, my voice rising.

'There is a procedure to be followed in such matters,' he chides me reproachfully. 'Even though I care for you very much, I had to follow the guidelines given to us for nabbing a killer red-handed. There are no short-cuts in such matters.'

I want to kill my knight in shining armour when he says this.

I recover and get ready to go back to Lucknow. I discover my suitcases have been neatly packed by Sujala and delivered to Samir's cottage. Samir and Vrinda drive me to the Coimbatore airport. Samir had wanted to accompany me all the way back to Lucknow but I have convinced him not to. We had one of our fights over it but I knew what I had to do in Lucknow, and I needed to do it on my own. Besides I don't want to bank on anyone's support anymore. Especially Samir's. I may never share with him how let down I have felt by his mother and him because I still feel a bit protective towards him. But deep down I know my friendship with him has cost me a lot. It's never going to be the same between us even though it feels wrong to blame him for the fate Mother met at the hands of Randeep.

I feel curiously light on the day I set out to meet the man in Lucknow. I had called him the previous night to fix an appointment. He had sounded excited on the phone, as if he was really keen to meet me. But his grim demeanour communicates something else when I enter his office. 'I learnt this morning that Randeep's lawyers have managed to get bail for him,' he informs me.

'I am not surprised,' I say making no attempt to hide the bitterness I feel at that moment. 'We are part of such a rotten system. You can get away with anything if you are rich and powerful.'

'You shouldn't be so pessimistic about the system, Things may take some time to reach their natural conclusion but justice does prevail in the end,' he pontificates as if he is addressing an election rally. I look away trying to hide my sarcastic smile but not before he notices it. A frown appears on his forehead.

'Do you need anything? Why did you want to meet me?' he asks and adds a little uncomfortably, 'I hope you are okay financially. Let me know if...' his voice trails off.

'She left all her money to me, you should know that,' I smile wryly and look away. There is no point in playing any more games with him.

'Are you my father?' I ask taking care to keep my face carefully averted.

He sounds shocked. 'Whatever gave you that idea?'

'Will you be very surprised if I told you that I believed you were my father until recently? Now I am not sure. That's why I came to meet you.'

'But surely your mother...?' he is once again finding it difficult to complete the sentence.

'She didn't tell me you were my father, but she never told me you weren't, either.'

He looks at me and then looks away. 'Neha, I met your mother when you were a year old. Your father had deserted her after one of those temple wedding ceremonies that lovers who eloped went through those days. Her family had long disowned her because they disapproved of the man she had fallen in love with. So she went and stayed with a friend when she was pregnant and prepared for the state civil services exams. She joined the services after you were born. I met her after she moved to Lucknow. I had been invited to her office as a chief guest during their annual day celebrations.'

I get up.

'Are you leaving?' he asks looking puzzled.

'I came to meet you with a question. You have given me the answer,' I tell him, blinking back tears. At the door I turn back and walk towards him again. He is looking out of his window. I know he is thinking of her.

'Thank you for everything,' I tell him, extending my hand.

He looks confused and holds my hand. His eyes are full of pain. 'Everything was for her,' he whispers. 'Do you know how much I miss her? She was so stubborn. So many times I asked her to employ a watchman but she thought whoever she hired would spy on her for me. As you know, we were having a lot of fights towards the end. I didn't mind her using me to earn commissions. But she had turned so grasping and indiscreet that I felt I had to step in at times. Turned out, I was right after all. If it wasn't for that side business of hers she would be alive today,' he concludes bitterly.

'I miss her too,' I tell him. 'When she was alive, there were times that I hated her. But it was wrong on my part to judge her. She was impossible and I think I used to be so angry with her because she could get away with anything.'

'You must leave now. You sound like her and today you also look so much like her. The way she used to be when I first met her,' he says, turning away.

I leave his room and the building and hail a rickshaw to get back home. When Jamuna opens the door I push her aside, run into my room and shut the door.

I allow the tears to flow only after making sure no one witnesses the abandon with which I surrender to them.

It's been two days since I met the man and I am still finding it difficult to get out of bed. I lie there and stare at the ceiling. If it wasn't for Jamuna's nagging I wouldn't even get up to have a bath. She gets all my meals on the bed, but I don't have an appetite. She calls for a physician but I lock my door and refuse to let him inside.

I miss Mother all the time. Worse, there is constant guilt gnawing at me. I have discovered that so much of her is within me these past few months. I am just an extension of her. It's difficult to tell where one begins and the other ends. Except I have discovered all this too late. It's almost as if the world outside knows I need this time and space to make sense of so many things. There have been no phone calls from anyone in the last two days.

It's only on the morning of my third day in bed that Veer calls to inform me there has been another murder. After he was granted bail, Randeep chose not to go back to Coimbatore for obvious reasons. Instead he had flown to Mumbai to stay in an apartment he owned there. He was shot dead early in the morning by unknown assailants. An investigation to track the murderers had been initiated.

'The Mumbai police is investigating the case. I may not have known about it if it wasn't for a batchmate of mine who's in the team of investigators. I had spoken to him from Coonoor once to find out for me how often Randeep used the apartment he had in Mumbai and he remembered that.' Veer is sounding excited as he shares the news.

'Who do you think killed him?' I ask.

'Well, my friend was saying the only lead they seem to have is that it could be the handiwork of a gang from UP. The way he was shot and the bullets recovered point to that. Now you tell me, who do you think could have masterminded his killing from Lucknow?' Veer counter-questions.

'I am glad he is dead,' is all I have to say.

Later I wonder whether I should call the man to thank him. But I know it's best if we stay away from each other. Mother was right, after all. In his own way, he is a good person and tries to do the right thing.

That night I sleep peacefully; no nightmares wake me up.

And let go

If it hadn't been for Veer, I would have never thought of going through what feels like an elaborate charade. The dead should be left in peace. Jamuna had suggested a shraad for Mother many times and I had always fobbed her off saying I wouldn't know how to go about doing something like that. But Veer has been persistent ever since Jamuna told him I have had no such ceremony after her death. He says it's important to have the rituals. Otherwise her soul will never know peace. He says it's just like me to have been so foolish. He insists on driving me to Allahabad on her second death anniversary and we are at the banks of the Sangam.

A priest with a small pyre in front of him chants mantras I don't understand. I find it soothing though, and from time to time smile at Veer who is sitting some distance away because the priest has told him to do so, on learning that he isn't family.

Suddenly the priest picks up a thin dry twig lying nearby and draws a face in the mud. It is the face of a woman. He asks me to stand and hands me a small brass vessel with milk in it.

'The body is gone, the soul is thirsty,' he says without looking at me. 'Please pour some milk into it,' he commands.

As I bend, my tears mingle with the milk to quench her thirst.

She can be at peace now.

Acknowledgements

Poorna, Sita, Revathi, Rohin, Abhay, Abhaya, Akhila, Sumaa and Madhukar for reading the manuscript and the invaluable feedback.

Thomas, Nandita and the team in Hachette India for their support.

Dipti and Dhruv for letting me write.

&

The town of Coonoor for the invitation it holds.